BEYOND ASPROMONTE

BEYOND ASPROMONTE
Being the Third Adventure of Burton the Red

by

Sandro Dariosto

per sempre Anita Edizione
Ferrara Seattle
2014

Printed in the United States of America

per sempre Anita Edizione
via delle Scienze 17 Ferrara

10 9 8 7 6 5 4 3 2 1

Beyond Aspromonte,
or
How Burton Survived the Night of the Thirteen Daggers

To the happy few

PROLOGUE

Two weeks ago I received a small packet in the mail from Italy addressed to me, Robert _____. Inside the brown padded envelope were a key, and a blank deposit slip from the central post office in Jesi. There was nothing else within the package. Not a note, not a word, not even an initial. But I recognized the hand which had addressed the outside. It was my brother's writing.

I tried for a few days to find him, calling everyone I knew, and got nowhere. No one had seen or heard from him for weeks, it turns out. But I learned one disturbing piece of news. His research fellowship at M_____ University had been continued, and they were expecting him in the fall, but he had failed to sign up for any classes during the registration period that opened the month before, and his Department Head a certain Dr. John McCabe mentioned that this was "just not like him," when I spoke with him on the phone. I knew that too. If anything, my brother has always been the overly organized one of the two of us. I'm the free agent, which has driven him crazy for years.

So after a long distance call to the Postal Inspector in Jesi, who told me only that "Yes, that is the number to a deposit box in our office," I took a plane to Rome. On the six or seven hour train ride from Termini to Jesi, jet lagged and nearly broke, I realized how angry I was with him. More than once I thought, 'You better be in some trouble,

1

Big Brother. If this is some prank, you will be in trouble when I find you.' But then, of course, I felt guilty about those thoughts immediately. I'd rather be angry with him, and spend a few days wandering around in Le Marche again, than be as worried as I am now, having found what I have found.

In Jesi, in the late afternoon, the inspector I spoke with on the phone, whose name is Umberto Tasso, took me into the safe. "You must be very worried," he said, as I described my situation again to him. He took the key and matched it with his and opened the safe deposit box. Inside was a long grey drawer, which Inspector Tasso extracted and then he led me to a little room where I could open the box in privacy. "Signor Roberto," he said, "let me know if I can be of any further assistance. My office is there, on the right. I will wait for you, and then we can lock up."

"Thank you, Inspector," I said as he closed the door to the little room with dusty gray shades discretely covering all the windows.

As I opened the lid on the box, there was a dry lump in my throat. After all we'd been through together, my brother and I, suddenly I was afraid to see what waited for me inside that box.

But it was just a red folder, and nothing else. Carefully tucked inside that red folder was a thick sheaf of plain white papers. There was a clasp on the upper right hand corner that held the pages all together, and I remembered that this was always my left-handed brother's way, to clip pages together like that. On the paper was his precise neat handwriting, covering both the front and back of every page. As always, he was being frugal. But before I began to read, I noticed something truly disturbing. On the first page, the backside of the document, his handwriting had dramatically changed. It was slanted drastically to the left, and the words were sometimes blended together. In fact, the very last paragraph was written as if it was one long word, without a break except at the end of a line, all the letters connected as if his pen never left the page. But he'd gone back then, after the fact, and put the punctuation marks in below the solidly handwritten lines. And then, printing so fiercely they often creased the paper, like he was scratching them on stone, he had made all the appropriate letters capitol. Perhaps what was most disturbing was that all of this, the punctuation, the fervently etched capitols, they were all of them perfectly correct. Even though the story he told was leading him into some intensely complex and convoluted sentence structures, all the punctuation was scrupulously correct.

Here then is what my brother wrote:

"He is on the run," Naguine told me. "As long as I've known him, he has always been on the run."

"But why?" I asked her. "He should be a hero in this country, I would think."

Naguine just stared at me for a long, quiet moment, and then she said, "Signore, do you know this country?"

I found her here outside of Jesi, living alone in an aluminum trailer parked by the train tracks. And her car, Rob, her car, I swear it is an old red Buick with a white soft top just like the one Burton drove back home with the circus. It can't be the same car, not here, not fifteen years later and halfway around the world. But it is his taste, isn't it? It's one of the ways I'm sure that he was here, that this is him again. That bright red Buick convertible pulling a shiny aluminum trailer. It had to be him. Rob, we're on his trail again. And we're getting close this time. I think.

It was easy to find her, even when I didn't know her name. You know, Jesi is not a big town, and it's a little out of the way. So you understand how it goes: I asked around for Burtoni in a few trattorias and coffee bars. He's easy to describe, what with the wheel chair and the red shirt, and the way he can get around. Before long, in a day or two, I had her name and I was looking for a traveler, a woman called Naguine, living completely alone.

In fact, it was all too easy, Rob. Too easy. And that tells me that when you were here, two years ago, Burton was here too. I think this is true, Rob. When you came straight up here from Siracusa, with Sister Teresa's letter in your back pocket, ignoring that job they wanted you to do in Texas, you found him. By God, Rob, you did it. But Jack Burton didn't want to be found then, Rob. He was here, he may even have seen you, but he didn't want to be found. And so he wasn't.

But he's long gone from Jesi now, I'll tell you, and that is why it was so damn easy for me to find Naguine. She's ready and waiting. She wants to tell his story.

I think it is because, like you and me, she misses him.

She says her name is Naguine, and everyone here calls her that. But this evening before I took her out to dinner (this is one way to get her to talk) I stole a glance into the glove box of the Buick. I was hoping to find Burton's name on the papers, Rob. But instead, I found hers. Her real name, I suppose. She is Sophia Ziegler, and there is a Bologna address under her name.

Naguine says that isn't her name, it is someone else who Burton knows and that this Buick is his car. I don't believe her. For some reason I don't understand yet, Sophia wants to remain invisible to the authorities. She wants to remain unknown, to be Naguine. Perhaps one night, when there has been enough wine at dinner, she'll tell me why.

5

This old trailer she lives in is tiny, but it is immaculate. Just one spotless room with a bed that folds into the wall and a table that is attached to an opposite wall, and two loose wooden chairs. Naguine survives now by taking in mending, and she does alterations. I think she drives around to all the little markets, from town to town, collecting the piecework and then returning it repaired and altered to her customers on her next round. So the back wall of her little trailer has a steel rod across it, and there hangs her work, all in a row.

Funny thing is, never once in all the time I've spent talking with her, never once has she had a piece of clothing in her hands. It all just hangs there waiting at the rear of the trailer.

I think it is because I came here asking about Burton. It's obvious she misses him, and talking about him brings Burtoni back to us for a while. That's what everyone here calls him, of course, Burtoni.

I think Naguine loves him.

But I don't think that love is returned.

It would be easy to see Burtoni's attraction to her, though. Naguine is a beautiful woman, still, wearing her fifty or so years very well. But we know about Rafaella Sciascia, about Burtoni's great love, lost forever as his heart was, in Sicilia. So I don't think, beautiful though Naguine is, Burton's interest lay in her.

How to describe her? You must come soon to see Naguine for yourself. I'm afraid, my brother, she is irresistible. But perhaps I say too much.

He face is shaped like a heart, with a tiny pointed chin under the wide expanse of her deep brown eyes. He skin is the rich color of an overripe peach, rosy but burnished, and she has a little black mole, just off center of that sweetly pointed chin, and it draws our eyes away from the perfect symmetry of her face. It is all framed by her wild brown hair, highlighted with the deep auburn dye she puts in it, lifting the rosiness of her skin until it seems to glow with its own light.

When she laughs, her eyes begin to spark like struck flint, and she laughs easily and with honest delight. The tears come to her eyes just as quickly, and she is comfortable enough with them to let them slip down her cheeks without wiping them away or trying to hide them. Her voice, when she speaks, has a music all its own, and her Italian is accented with the sounds of other languages I can't identify, so her words draw you in like her eyes.

It is hard to imagine a man who would be invulnerable to her charms. I don't think Burton was, not entirely. Yet there is something else, perhaps a greater attraction than Naguine's own earthly beauty here, something else would draw Burton here, I'm sure.

But I'm getting ahead of myself.

You see, after dark in the late evenings, long after we'd finished eating and we'd drunk away all the wine, and once we are deeply involved in telling our stories about Il

Rosso, the great Burtoni, Naguine always does something I know you'll recognize, Rob. From a drawer hidden in the floorboards of the Buick, she extracts a small, carved wooden box. Inside it is her pipe in two pieces, long and thin and ivory, with a tiny bowl like a thimble. When the memories of Burtoni are present enough, and her eyes well up with tears, she fills it with that black brown paste in the box and smokes it, just one pipeful or maybe two. After a while, her damp eyes grow blank and the memories continue.

Though she feels comfortable enough to smoke in front of me, Naguine never offers any of it. Never once. In fact, the way she handles it, she seems to say it is too precious for me to even dare to taste.

But I know you remember the sweet, pungent smoke in the tent by the circus, and Jack Burton and his trained ape imbibing as he spun his stories at us, as we two children looked on and listened.

I believe this is Naguine's true attraction for Jack Burton, the dulcet world of the pipe. This is why Burton with his broken heart, wanders here into the byways of Le Marche. It is not love, but the relief the pipe grants him from living so long with his old soul and all his endless losses.

I suspect, somewhere deep down, Naguine realizes this too. Her Burtoni is a lost and wandering soul, with no real love left in his heart, no room for love, except of course for his love of Rafaella. Forever. And with only the pipe to grant him peace.

Naguine must know, as you and I know, as Sister Teresa knows, how old a soul he is.

*   *   *

"I believe it goes back to Aspromonte, and what happened there," Naguine told me. She was lounging on the bed in the dark one night or another, after she'd smoked a pipeful of her sweet brown tar. She said to me, "But Burtoni doesn't think that. He always says that it was what happened in Castellnotte. Not at Aspromonte."

With a thin waft of smoke drifting before her eyes, she tried to explain to me what Jack Burton believed, and why he was wandering and wandering so. It was what happened at Castellnotte, this is what he believed. "The people down there in Sicily, they have long, long memories," Naguine said to me. "Burtoni believes the picciotti down there are hunting for him, still hunting for him after all these years. And he still fears their black hands."

Naguine exhaled slowly the last of the white smoke she held in her lungs. "But I would say to him, 'Burtoni, how can you be so sure?'" With all the stories he told about what happened in the mountains of Calabria, all his talk about the foolish battle at Aspromonte. "How can you be sure, I would say to him, it's not all about Aspromonte?"

Naguine let her hand rest back on the pillow that night, her rich dark hair surrounding the diamond of her face in the dim light, with the smoke raising clouds behind her eyes, and she told me all about Jack Burton's fears.

"'How can you be sure?' I would ask him. He would only mutter his answer. "Castellnotte, my dear, Castellnotte. This is where it all starts.'" And so, on one night or another, Naguine told me his story.

* * *

They were in bed, arguing, because he was haunted by all his memories, until she objected and said to him, "So tell me, Gianni Burtoni, why did the stabbing occur when it did?"

It made him angry that she brought it up, because clearly he didn't want to consider what he knew to be true. 'The third of August,' he muttered, though it bothered him to speak of it.

"One year to the day," Naguine said. All she really wanted to do was embrace him, to hold him until his demons went away. But instead she pressed the point. 'It happened on the first anniversary, exactly to the day, one year after the attack at Aspromonte," she said.

He was silent. He wanted to object, he wanted her to be wrong and he wanted to be angry with her, with the whole world. But what he was, was silent.

"Gianni Burtoni, my dearest," she said to him, and ran her hand along his soft bearded cheek. "You know these people, Gianni. You know how they think, you know how it works. They did not pick that day for nothing. It was no accident."

He didn't answer for the longest time, he just maneuvered himself with those strong arms of his so he was turned away from her. After a while, he just said, "It wasn't only that."

I didn't interrupt Naguine that evening, I only listened and let her journey through the smoke, doing all the talking, though I didn't follow much of what she told me. Still I asked not one question, because I didn't want to stop the flow of words and memories. Before long, in the daylight, I let her tell me what happened at Aspromonte. She spoke easily, and in the afternoon, with no wine or narcotic to help, because she liked this story, because it made a sense to her, a sense that kept Burton safe in the world. It was an explanation, and explanations, whatever else they are, they are a comfort.

The beginning of this story always made Burtoni smile.

"They sent us all home," he would say, with that little, proud grin of his. "After the handshake at Teano, after the General handed over the whole of Southern Italy, from Naples clear to Marsala, after he gave his whole new and free empire to the King from Piedmonte, Vittorio Emmanuele, then they were afraid of us, little Naguine. The Thousand. We were just a ragtag bunch of lads in red shirts carrying the old worn out muskets they gave us, and still they were afraid of us."

Burtoni would stop there and laugh out loud about that. "We'd marched from Marsala to Naples, through Calatafimi and Milazzo and we'd sailed across the straits of Messina, riding on a streak of luck and a lot of little tested courage. But mainly we counted on the cowardice of the Bourbons, and they rarely let us down, girl, rarely.

"So after Teano, Cavour and his boys up north, they were afraid of us. 'On to Roma, and the Pope,' we'd be shouting. We were ready to press forward, and I think, Naguine, they believed that if we took Rome, we might have made the General into our King. That's what Cavour and his clever diplomats were really afraid of, Naguine, they were all afraid of the Generalissimo.

"So after Teano, after the handshake that gave it all over to the King, Vittorio Emanuele and Cavour sent us up north somewhere, to keep us quiet.

"But Corrao and I didn't go. Giovanni said to me, 'They're trying to bury us up there in the snows. I'm a southern lad, Burtoni. I'm not going.'

"So we went back to Palermo, Giovanni Corrao and I, because he knew a place in the Albergheria where we could stay."

Naguine winked at me, then, and said, "That means old Corrado kept a lady back down there." She chuckled at that, but I knew too that Burton must have gone back there hoping to find Rafaella Crisiana again. From reading those old journals of his we were given in Siracusa, I know, he must have been hoping to find his Rafaella, and to make it all right with her. And either Naguine didn't know this, or she didn't want to know it.

* * *

They lived in the Albergheria for a year, that time. He worked now and then on fishing boats, and sometimes he sold fish in the Vucciria. Burton did just enough to get by. And old Corrao, he became Dottore Calogero again, and people came to him all the time for his cures and his powders.

I suppose, Rob, that the main part of his 'cures and powders' had a lot to do with that little brown paste both Naguine and Burton kept hidden around them. Don't you think this must have been when Jack Burton discovered the pipe? It was probably his friend Dottore Calogero, a.k.a. Signor Corrado, or, as history knows him now, General Giovanni Corrao, it was he who introduced Burton to the sweet smoke of that pipe. That was when he started, Rob, to quell the pain already in his heart, to kill the hard memories of all he'd lost.

Naguine told me more, Rob. Burton and Dottore Calogero were waiting down there in Palermo, I think. And the General didn't let them wait for long. Burton claimed that nearly a year passed like that, working and taking life gently in Palermo. But when the heat of the summer came back again, they began to hear rumors of the General's return. There was no Rosalino Pilo now to spread the gossip, so the word wandered out on its own, arriving with every ship that sailed into the port of Palermo, and it came wandering down from the mountains above the Conca d'Oro, where the contadini and the picciotti were waiting too. Il Generale will come, soon, they all kept hearing it on the northern winds. But they didn't know who or what to believe. How could they know?

But then real news came. The General had made a speech, the newspapers said, in Locarno, calling for Rome and Venice to be free. That was the first we heard of it. But even Corrao and Burton believed it then. After all, there was no Pilo out there in the world to make it all up. So they began to wait and to watch and to listen differently to the rumors on the wind.

In Palermo, then, some of the people, the old aristocrats mainly, spoke of separation. Sicilia must be free, she is her own land. In the trattorias at night in the Albergheria, back then, daggers would flash and there were fights in the alley and streets. "Rome and Venice," one side would say. "Free Sicilia," another would yell. And then the blood of brothers would spill on the stones again.

It was the old aristocrats, still sitting on all their land, with all their old estates, and the churchmen too, with all their old influence and their favorites. They used this strife, playing brother against brother, while they sat on all the property, on all their heaps of wealth.

But then, almost like a dream, the General finally did arrive. Burton would always pull himself up taller in his chair to tell Naguine about those days. "O sweet Naguine," he would mutter, "I remember the day well. The 27th of June, it was. He arrived as if from nowhere, Little One, without any warning, like a god descending from the heavens above. Like a mystery from deep in the flowered earth, Naguine. There in the Piazza beside La Martorana he stood, O Naguine, his blonde hair flowing in the breeze, one of this boots up on a stair as if he were ready to rush on the palazzi of the rich, his arm flung out to the growing and cheering crowd. And he was wearing the red shirt again, by god, Naguine, the Red Shirt again."

When Burton told her this the first of many times, he wasn't wearing any shirt at all. He was sitting up in bed, his bare back all hard and brown from the sun, the muscles in his arms tensed with his excitement. But he touched his chest as if he were wearing that red shirt, and it was almost as if Naguine could see it. "Il Generale didn't really need to speak, Naguine. That Red Shirt blazoned again on his back, and his stance on the stairs, poised to leap forward into the future. It didn't matter what he said, Naguine. That Red Shirt said everything that could be said."

To Rome and Venice, was his cry. That was all they heard, and all they needed to hear.

When Corrao and Burton appeared, they were among the first lieutenants at his side. But it was to Burton the General spoke first. Though Corrao was standing right beside him, with an old musket in his hand, the General shouted, "Il Rosso!" and laughing he clasped Burton's hand. The two of them embraced then, and holding him reminded Burton of how small and frail the General truly was, how the years were wearing on him since they'd first sailed the Atlantic together. He was growing old, Burton thought. It was hard to feel it in the frailty of his bones, because when he stood there on the stairs of La Martorana, he seemed so strong and tough, he seemed invincible again and it seemed they would have him forever. But Burton remembered the rheumatism in the General's bones, and the way he'd limped into Lugano and how Burton had nursed him to health again in Switzerland back in '48.

As Naguine spoke of this, she paused and looked away from me then. She said, "The strength in my dear Burtoni seemed to fail and weaken, right at that moment, as he went on talking to me about the General growing old. He said, 'Soon enough we would all see how frail Il Generale was at Aspromonte.'" Then Burton fell silent, and would tell her no more, not until later, when she asked him again on another day, and they argued again, about everything and nothing, and again in the dark of night.

*   *   *

On a different night, when his spirits were higher, when the fire in his eyes returned, Burton told Naguine more. "At first, it was like our ride with Rosalino," he said. There they were, riding across the mountains and the plains of Sicily, gathering men to the General's side as they went. "But, Rosalino is gone now, Naguine, gone like so many others."

"It was different that time, Naguine," Burton would say. This was in the height of the Sicilian summer, and it was hot as hell itself when they rode down out of the Peloritani Mountains. But in some ways it was easier too, for now the men seemed to sprout up as if out of the earth itself, joining them as they marched along like the harvest from seeds planted the season before.

By the time they reached Catania, they had grown to thousands strong. It was not just the Thousand, no. They were thousands upon thousands, and more were joining them with every day. "To Rome and Venice," was all the cry. "To Rome and Venice." So many of them together, that suddenly the General had a new problem.

"'Once again, as they did two years before, they had the sea to cross. How was he to get an Army of five thousand and more Red Shirts across the Straits of Messina? This was the problem. When they marched into Catania, more than 5,000 strong, the city rejoiced and the crazed celebrations began, the lights of the city burned all night, with bonfires in the streets, and the dancing and singing didn't die down until almost dawn. And all of it because the General had arrived. But there was other news, too. You see, old King Vittorio Emanuele had declared them all outlaws and rebels. And from Genova, General Cialdini was sailing south with sixty battalions of the new Royal Italian Army to stop them. The Army of Italia had launched her ships against them, against the General who had given birth to their country.

It was Giovanni Corrao who told Burton that news, for he had been with the General when that message from the north was delivered. And it was hard news that meant civil war, Italian against Italian, on the battlefield, brother against brother. Suddenly their cries of Roma! and Venezia! seemed shallow indeed, and touched with an evil bitterness.

So there was hesitation, Burton said. It followed hard upon all the rejoicing of their arrival, and that long night of revels behind them. But after a few hours sleep alone in his room the General emerged, his eyes tired and his walk still arthritically stiff. Yet he held his head high. He said to them all, "We must act quickly, my friends! It must be now!" What he meant, Burton told Naguine, was that with General Cialdini bearing down on them, they could not wait and be caught on this side of the Straits. They needed to cross immediately to Calabria, with as many of their 5,000 as they could muster, and as soon as they could. You see, the General never really believed that it would come to civil war. When the confrontation came, when they in their Red Shirts met the battalions of Cialdini on the field, brother would not shoot brother down. The General believed that in their hearts, whatever uniform they wore, they all knew that Rome was their Capitol, and Venice was the home of their hearts.

"Roma o Morte!" the General said to them, to just a few of them in the room. But it became their battle cry. And it drove them on.

"Roma o Morte!" Burton shouted. He cried out that night so many years later, at the memories of Catania, and

17

the crossing to come. But it was into the moonlit shadows of Naguine's bedroom in Le Marche that he cried. "Roma o Morte!"

So in the morning they commandeered two ships lying in the Port of Catania, an Italian frigate who joined them without resistance, and a French merchant marine they took at gunpoint. The old sailor who lay lurking in the General's heart, he showed his salty hand, and he took control of this new, pirated navy. They were a little piecemeal, and yet they were bold. They were the Navy of the Red Shirts of the Italian Republic, they were, by God. Pirates in red shirts, they were. They filled the two barques with as many men as they would hold, and set sail across the Straits. And they landed at Melito, Burton said, at the same sure place where they had come ashore two years before. "So you see, my dear Little One," Burton whispered to Naguine across the rumpled bed sheets, "almost exactly two years later, we landed at Melito to complete our unfinished task."

Roma o Morte! was on all their lips, as they disembarked and, just as the Thousand had done in '60, they marched straight up into the mountains of Calabria. I suppose there were, then, only two or three thousand of them, for not all of them could make that first crossing in just two ships. But they couldn't wait for the whole force to gather. And they believed that like it had been back in '60, the people would rise up with them and march on with them to Rome, where the people of Rome would hand over the

18

city, while the Pope with his French protectors would flee. But I'm afraid, brother Rob, I'm afraid they were wrong. The General, too. All of them, they were all so wrong. It was the first sign they had that the world was different. It was only a few years later, but everything had changed.

My guess, Rob, it was the priests who got to them. Because you see, they were marching on the Pope this time, and not the Bourbon King of Spain. When they cried out as they marched along, "Roma o Morte!" they meant to take the eternal city right out of the Pope's hands. Burton always believed it was the priests who worked against them then, who hardened the people's hearts into papal stones.

But whoever or whatever it was, they marched up into the mountains with precious few Calabrians joining them. They were moving quickly, because they knew Cialdini was coming for them. For two days and a night, they marched in the summer heat, and with not even a bite to eat. And still no one joined them in any numbers. Almost no one. And only a straggler or two along the way met them, and not even one child ever offered them a tiny taste of food. Not even one.

And so, after that long hungry march across the mountains, the General pulled them up on the broad, high plain at Aspromonte, and there they rested. Some of the Red Shirts roamed out and returned with a few head of sheep. Without wasting a precious shot, they slaughtered and roasted them. And so they ate and rested, but it was food they took, not food given to them, just food needed to feed a tired army before it could ready itself for the march on to the capitol.

And when the marauding soldiers came back with the sheep, they returned with news, too. You see, they all believed in their hearts that the Pope would abandon Rome when they marched within sight of Lazio. But Cialdini had landed his battalions at Napoli, in order to cut them off as

19

they maneuvered to the North. The Italian forces were waiting for them there: Cialdini's sixty battalions.

And yet, there was worse news too. The Royal Army of Calabria was now advancing ahead of Cialdini's men, marching toward them under some colonel named Pallavicino. He led just six or seven battalions toward them now, but he would intercept the Red Shirts in days, if not in hours. He was coming, and he was closing in.

"We will have to meet this Colonel here," the General announced to his assembled officers. And so Corrao and Burton marshaled their positions, and they waited for this man Pallavicino and his little Calabrian battalions. Still they were all sure in the depths of their hearts that the regulars would fail to attack. Certainly these common soldiers would come to, they would awaken, once they faced one another on the field of battle, with the General between them. "Fire not one shot," the General ordered them all in the assembly. "Not one shot!" Then he strolled from one corps to the next corps, shouting out to them all the same simple order.

"Stand your ground. But fire not one shot," he shouted his orders to the men. "Not one shot!"

*   *   *

"Why does Burtoni always call you his 'Little One'?"
I asked Naguine.

We were sitting at an open fire outside the silver trailer late on a warm and sultry night. I was pouring some fine verdicchio that we had set beside us in a tub of cool river water, and it's dry sweetness went down well and easy, and I suppose we were deep into the second bottle then. There was nothing but stars and the low firelight, and sometimes in the dark night, Naguine would sing in her deep, warm voice, in a language I couldn't quite place in the world. It seemed to come from everywhere, but always somewhere far away.

She smiled when I asked her that question, and a length of her black hair fell loose across her face, hiding that smile for a moment. When she pushed her hair back the firelight caught her face again, and I could see that her teeth were parted just a little, so the pearl of her smile was nearly a laugh, it was so joyful.

With her head tilted forward toward me, and that pretty mole on her pointed chin, and that nearly laughing grin on her lips, she reached a hand out and touched my wrist. Her touch was warm too, and she seemed—maybe this is just the verdicchio talking—she seemed just a girl. "His little one."

But she didn't really ever laugh. She just held that strange parted smile as she spoke. "My husband was a guitar player," she whispered. Her dark brown eyes caught the firelight and seemed to shine like water in the moonlight. "No," she said. Then her brown gaze looked away from me to somewhere, and I felt the loss. "He was the greatest guitar player of our time," she said, out loud now. "People came from far and wide, from all over the world to hear him. We lived then, our whole family, and three other families, in a camp like this just outside of Paris. And every night he would walk into the city to play in the cafes. When he returned in a taxi in the morning, there was money, oh money galore, in his pockets. And all of us, his family and all the others, I suppose there were thirty or forty of us then, we ate and lived well. We had everything we wanted, anything we desired, and more, all because of his guitar."

Naguine moved over to sit next to me then, as if she was cold, though the night was warm. She put one arm around me, and I nestled into her side, my face burning where her hair touched it. "I know," she said to the fire, "you're wondering why, if we had so much, why we lived in a camp outside of town. But this is how we lived, this is what we loved. My husband's guitar bought us all the freedom to live together, in our own way. This was our dream.

"It all happened back between the wars, in the 20's and 30's, when there were still so many of us around, and we could move around the way we loved to move around, freely. You see, when the leaves started to fall in Paris and the winter winds would begin to blow through Paris, we just packed up our things and wandered down here into Italy. My husband and his guitar were so famous then, we would all stop at Nizza, and he would play there in the casinos and cafes, and when the cold worked its way down and arrived there on the coast of Provence, we would just pack up our things and drift down to Bari or Capri, or sometimes into Spain, down to Barcelona and then all the way to Valencia, or even Cadiz if the winter was hard. We jut followed the warmth of the sun, and lived on the six strings of his guitar. It was a beautiful life. So easy and so beautiful, it was all a dream."

"But when does Burtoni come into this?" I said, more to keep her soft body close to me than to find out about Jack Burton, even though I wanted to know.

"He came the first time when we were staying in Paris. I think he heard my husband playing in the Can-Can or the Bal Tabarde, I really can't remember which. But dear Burtoni was so intoxicated with the music, Will, he followed my husband all the way home to our camp one morning, after a very long night in the cafes. And we all loved Burtoni in an instant, well, you know how he is. Big and bellowing and full of stories and full to the brim with love. He was gadjo, you know, but he was more like one of us. He was a traveler, too, in his heart if not his blood.

"I think it was partly the way he loved the music. But it was also partly because he didn't have a home. You know, Will, he belongs to the world, not to any place in the world. He moved where he wanted to, or where ever the world sent him.

"It was only later, after my husband died, that I found out he wasn't really like us. No, he was running away, he was moving around to stay invisible. He is different than I am, he just seemed the same to me back then. The life of the road is not the same for everyone.

"What is he running from?" I asked her, forgetting for that moment that the old Nun had sent us here to kill him. But now Naguine was holding my hand in one of hers, and I forgot everything else.

"This is why I'm telling you these stories. Only because you seem to love him too," Naguine said, then she took a sip from the glass of verdicchio in her other hand. "You fool," she added, just a little too late.

"But . . . " I wanted to object to something about this, though I'm not sure now what it was.

Then she rested her hand on my shoulder, and though she is twice my age, I just wanted her to stay there beside

23

me for as long as possible. "Burtoni was younger then, you know. He did not look so old as he does now. But he was new to his wheelchair back then. He didn't get around in it like he can move around now."

"New to the chair?" I said. "But how?" I said.

Naguine ignored me, saying only, "I can't tell you every story at once." She laughed a little then, through those parted teeth and that lovely smile.

I should have objected, I know. I want to know how he wound up in that wheel chair, what happened to him. But you must understand, Naguine was there beside me, and her hair was draped gently over my shoulder, and the firelight and the stars were bright, and the verdicchio was so sweet and dry at once.

She just went on. "So that first morning when he came home to our camp with my husband, when the light rose and it was time to sleep, Burtoni needed help. He was having trouble getting into his chair, from out of the cab they came in. Now he didn't want any help, though my husband and the driver tried to offer him a hand. He pushed them away.

"But his chair rolled a little, and he was going to fall, I thought. So I just ran toward him and braced the chair with all my strength, and Burtoni smiled over at me, lifting himself into it, and said, 'Thank you, my little one.'

"I think he let me help him because I was just a little girl then. I was still a little child, so he looked at me, with my grimaced up face and my shoulders all pressed tight against the back of that chair to hold it steady, with all my slight weight behind it, and Burtoni chuckled as he hoisted himself over into the seat.

"His arms were strong, you know, but not as strong as they are now. He was, like I told you, new to this chair then, and the strength in his arms was not what it has become.

24

"'Thank you, my little one,' he said, and then he touched my face on the chin. He brushed his big rough thumb gently right here," Naguine touched that pretty dark mole on her chin, the one that draws your eyes to her face and to the dark angles of her eyes.

"Later in the morning, when the music and talk died down and everyone was falling asleep, I held his chair steady again so he could lie down and stretch out on a blanket to sleep under the noonday sun alongside us. You see, our life then was like a dream. 'Good night, my little one,' Burtoni said to me, though it was the middle of his day.

"So ever since I was just a little girl, he has called me his 'little one.' As long as I have known him, no matter how old and drear I grow, I'm always his 'Little One.'"

That was when I made my mistake, Rob. I said, "But you were married."

Naguine stared over at me from under her lifted brows, as if to ask, 'So?'

"How old were you?" I demanded.

"I was ten, maybe eleven then. I'm not really sure, just now."

"What was your husband the guitar player called?" I asked, though she knew I meant to ask her how she could be married and a child at the same time.

Naguine answered my real question, and ignored the one I asked. "Among us, the marriages are always arranged. And they are arranged and set when we are very young. So, yes, I was married when I was nine or so, partly because I was growing up so fast. And mostly because, well, look who was my husband. Any family would like to marry a daughter to a great man like he was."

I tell you now, Rob, in all of these conversations, over a month's time, never once did she use her husband's name. I think I asked again that night who he was, but that was the last time. I sensed, before long, Rob, that Naguine would not use his name. She would not speak it out loud. Instead she would go around and around awkwardly in her sentences to always just say 'him' or 'he' or at most 'my husband.' I think it is some sort of superstition, Rob, some belief that to say his name aloud would disturb his soul., so I just stopped asking, and let it rest at that.

Naguine laid her head on my shoulder then, and she whispered softly, "We were not married that way you think, you little American fool. No, I was just a little girl, still pure of heart and soul. We were not married, not the way you are thinking, not for several more years. It was not like that." She put all the stress on her last word, and I understood it was the first of her invitations to me. It wouldn't, Rob, be the last.

On another night, sitting together under the Le Marche stars, Naguine went on with Jack Burton's story. Or maybe it all was the same evening, I can't be sure anymore. My brief time with her is all blended and mired in the detritus of my mind. She said to me, "One night, when Burtoni and I were both awake in bed, when he couldn't sleep because of all his memories, and I was stroking his forehead like this and comforting him," Naguine let her gentle fingers flutter through the hair brushing my forehead like a soft breeze. "He told me the rest of what happened at Aspromonte. I suppose because he was still troubled by it.

Burton said to Naguine, "Remember, the General had commanded us, 'Not one shot!' So we waited on the broad plain in the low mountains, as Pallavicino and his six battalions of Royal Troops approached us from the west."

There were so many youngsters with them on that battlefield, on both sides of the field. They were just boys really, who had not seen the fierce action at Milazzo or made the bold charge at Calatafimi, so many who had never even seen a battle before. They were jumpy, and excited, and more than a little afraid, on Pallavicino's side, as on that of the Red Shirts.

You see, after the great triumph of the Thousand, after they'd marched clear from Marsala to Capova, all across the South, after that there were many, many more than a thousand men in Sicily and Calabria who strutted around and claimed to have been with the Thousand. If everyone who ever claimed to march with the Generalissimo back in '59 had really been there at his side, the Red Shirts would have been 100,000 strong.

But what all that really meant is when the General returned to Palermo crying out, "Roma o Morte!" suddenly all the talk stopped. Every braggart and every boy who'd claimed to be among the Thousand, and even the ones who'd only claimed they dreamed of marching with the General, but responsibilities, mothers and sisters and families had held them back, now suddenly they all had to show what they were truly made of. "So you see, dear little Naguine," Burton said to her, "we had thousands of lads on our side of that long plateau at Aspromonte who were both scared to death, and didn't know themselves what they would do when the real fighting, and not the bragging, began."

For Colonel Pallavicino it was probably even worse. More than likely even his veterans in the Royal Army of Calabria had never seen a moment of action, they'd only seen the parade grounds in Caserta and Benevento. They'd never, most of them, faced oncoming fire, or the charge of anything even a little like a thousand Red Shirts.

Burton stopped there, and his eyes suddenly filled with tears at what he was about to tell her. "I don't think I can go on," he muttered, his head hanging down, his eyes shielded from her gaze. He was in such pain, just within his memories alone, and he whispered their names to himself, "Francesco. Rosalino." Naguine tried to comfort him with an embrace, and with kisses. "All gone," he whispered. "Antonio. Matteo. Gone." She showered him with kisses, and she offered him more than that. Naguine thought that surely she could distract him, but it was no use. He was in real pain, all these many years later. "My lost Rafaella,' he whispered over and over again, his face twisted with regrets. "My lost Rafaella." He kept repeating her name, and then Naguine was afraid for him. She was afraid, and she could tell me no more of his story.

She got up and left my side by the fire then. She stood up without saying another word, and I suspected it was all over for that night. But I sat there anyway, gazing at the dwindling flames alone, drinking the last of the verdicchio. It had grown dark and late, and Jack Burton seemed far, far away and strangely unimportant in the world.

But in a little while Naguine emerged from her silver trailer, and walked silently across the darkness toward me. She wore a scarf now, royal blue with some kind of pattern of deep red and dark green running through it, but I couldn't understand the patterns in the low firelight, and in the way she wore it wrapped around her head like a veil. When she came close, she looked at me blankly, and her eyes were glassy and deep, catching the flames from the ground. She seemed relaxed, and her face in the dim light was a pure olive, without a wrinkle or a crease. In her calm, she seemed younger, nearly a girl again, I suppose, all the worry and care of the years gone now.

She nestled next to me and I put my arm around her, as if to make a refuge she didn't need. But she rested against me anyway.

"I gave him some of this that night," she said, and from out of the folds of that deep blue scarf, she pulled her little wooden box. "And then he was able to tell me the rest of what happened." She set the intricately carved box in her lap, with both her hands around it, safely tucked away from even my touch. She never offered to even open it for me, but I know that she had gone away from me to smoke from it, alone and out of my sight. And this was how she seemed so young that night, how beautiful it made her, that sweet smoke of youth and gentleness.

I knew, even then, that if I asked to share it, to have a try at it, the smallest taste, she would say no and never. "You are young, and you are just playing with it." I knew this is what she would tell me. "It is too powerful for you. It would swallow up a young fool like you. When you are a hundred years old, and you've seen children dying in battle, over causes that don't exist, over lies told about the moon by leaders with wide sincere moonfaced eyes, then you come find me. But now," she would laugh at me, "now you have no use for this. It has only a use for you."

So I didn't say a word that night, I just sat with my arm wrapped around her, and she with her hands folded around the little box, and she seemed young and ageless, and the night could last forever, I dreamed.

"The boy's name was Matteo, if I remember it right. Burtoni told me his story that night, after we smoked and it had cleared and rested his mind.

This Matteo was just a lad, Burton told her. He had a mop of curly brown hair that sprang around his head like a halo. And his hazel green eyes were as bright as his laughter. And his smile, it was broad and flashed easily across his face, and it was filled with his white, crooked teeth, big and sparkling. Burton sighed then as he said, "He was just a lad, my dear Naguine. Only a boy."

Matteo was born up north, around Vignola, where they grow the sweet cherries that made his cheeks so red. He'd joined the Royal Italian Army, as soon as he could lie about his age and get away with it, because he was filled with talk about the General, il Generalissimo, he'd say. But the King and his counselors sent Matteo off to Palermo, to be like a policeman in restless Sicilia. So ironically, though the King had tried to bury his kind, Matteo was in Palermo when the General arrived. Matteo was there to hear him singing out, "Roma o morte!"

Once he heard the General speak that day in the piazza, Matteo deserted. He hung onto just his rifle and his pants, but that was about it, you see. He showed up in Corrao's face, tearing his shirt from off his own back, and demanding of Burton, "Give me the Red Shirt!"

Well, the lad was so sweet and sincere, it was impossible to turn him down. So they got him a shirt and a belt, and soon he was shouting "Roma o Morte!" with the best of them. He was one of the first recruits.

Matteo marched with them all the way across that island. And then on through the three days of hunger to

Aspromonte. And so there he stood, on the plateau of Aspromonte, he and a few thousand like him on either side, as Pallavicino's battalions came toward them, and then they began to fire at them.

But the General stood before all of them on that plain, his arms outstretched, and he cried out, "Not a Shot!" And still the Royal battalions came marching forward, and the scattering of fire on the other side began to grow. The General stood in his simple Red Shirt, with his blonde hair tossed back in the breeze, and he kept crying out to them all, to both sides of the lines, "Hold fast!" In his heart, he believed that when the King's battalions charged, they would just be swallowed by an embrace.

"Fraternize," Corrao muttered under his breath, in disbelief. They weren't going to fight. He stood beside Burton, and the General with his arms spread out was just before them, with his back to the enemy, proclaiming with his stance that they were not our enemies, they were all countrymen, they were brothers in arms.

It seemed crazy as Pallavicino's men moved toward them, and I think in some places their line collapsed and the Red Shirts began to fire back. But it was all, for a moment, still scattered and strange, unlike any battle Burton had ever seen. And there they stood, so near to the General, none of them would dare to even raise their arms. "But still, my Little One, Pallavicino and his men kept marching toward us" Burton said. At some point, I think, those young lads in the Royal lines must have been emboldened by the way the Red Shirts stood there so still, bright shining targets not responding, as if they weren't even human.

Burton could see the buttons on their blue uniforms glinting in the sun, and the sweat streaming off the Generalissimo's brow under the August sun, and he thought even then, at that moment, that maybe there were tears welling in his eyes, and not the tears of a General.

31

Matteo, youngster that he was, he could stand it no more. As if in a fit, he broke ranks, with all his heart and his courage overwhelming him, he charged forward a few steps, lifting the fine rifle the King's armorer had given him. But he was pointing it now at the King's men.

Our General moved toward him, his arms out, ordering, "No! Halt!" But at the lifting of his rifle, Matteo began to take on fire. "No!" my General called out. There was a crackle of a dozen guns from the Royal lines, and Matteo went down on his knees. "As the General was reaching for him, I saw what I could not then believe, my Naguine, my sweet Little One," said Burton. "I find it hard to believe this, even now, even a whole lifetime later."

Burton had stood bedside him in the streets of Palermo, he'd ridden with him out of Morazzone and led him to Lugano when he was ill, and he'd charged behind him across the bridges at the fortress of Milazzo. He'd seen him standing tall and fearless, under heavy fire, with bullets and shrapnel hurtling past where the rest of the rebels hid. Though Burton had never thought of it so clearly, not until that moment, I guess he believed the General was free in some powerful way, the General couldn't be touched. The rest of them, all just mortal lads belabored by fear, they could fall and die at his side, or be wounded permanently and vitally, but he,
their General, he seemed impervious to it all. He was as untouchable as he was fearless. But Burton was wrong. This belief of his, though nebulous and unclear, was just foolishness. They all were wrong. Aspromonte taught us all that.

*   *   *

Old Jack Burton fell silent for a moment then. He looked up at the heavens above them, though he was lying beside Naguine in her bed. It was as if he was seeing it all happen again in his memory, in ways he couldn't ever escape. Then, just as suddenly as he had ceased speaking, he began again.

"O Naguine, as the General stepped toward the fallen Matteo, trying to lift him, a bullet ripped through the thigh of his pants. I saw it bite, like a pitch of light, and in a blink, the blood was streaming down his pant leg. He never winced, or paused, he just strode forward, hoping I think to pull Matteo back up onto the lad's feet."

It was too late. The General had been hit. His blood, his impossible blood, was staining the ground. And sunny, young Matteo was on his knees in the short grass. And so, the hot burn of anger rose up from Burton's gut, and under the Royal fire, he lifted his Musket, ready to return their fire and to charge at the bastards who threatened to down him, his Generalissimo.

But Giovanni Corrao stood beside him. The same Corrao who had moaned at the order to hold their fire, who had scoffed at the thought of fraternizing with enemy brothers. It was he. Giovanni Corrao saw Burton lifting the musket to his shoulder, and whatever Corrao believed, he followed the General's orders. "Jack!" he said, calling him by his English name. "No, Jack!" he said. It was strange to hear that English word come from him.

Then Corrao reached up with both his hands, and snatched the barrel of Burton's cool musket, pulled it away from him. Burton clung to the musket stock at first, but Giovanni Corrao was stronger than him, by far, and he just pulled the gun away, right out of Burton's grip. But in desperation, in that brief struggle, the gun went off. The force of Corrao's hands jerking it away from the twisted grip of Burton was enough, that he pulled the trigger. "Remember that, Little One," Burton said to Naguine. "It was I who pulled that trigger, Naguine. Not Giovanni. It was not Giovanni Corrao. It was I."

For a moment, then he stood, with his hands in front of himself, empty. Corrao smoothly slipped Burton's musket into his ready grip. And then, like it was a spell, like it was all imagined, a dream, the scattering of fire died away in front of them. Pallavicino's men, at least the men just before them, in the front of the lines, they held their fire. The battlefield all around them fell silent.

Burton confessed to her, "I don't know that it was my shot. It could easily have come from the Royal lines, or some say now it was just a ricochet, from a rock or a tree. I will never know if it was my shot, but I can tell you this, Naguine, it was at that very moment, the exact moment of my shot, that he went down."

The General had leaned over to reach for Matteo on the ground, when the bullet, no, that's not right. When Burton's bullet tore into the General's ankle. This time it was no flesh wound in the thigh, drawing sacred blood. No this time the bullet ripped through all those delicate bones, shattering the ankle like so much thistle and grass, and down the Generalissimo fell.

At first, no one was sure what had happened, in all the excited fray. But the lines of the Red Shirts, and the Royal lines facing them, they all saw one thing. They saw the great, impervious General crumble to the ground, and lay bleeding now in the grass. And they saw Giovanni Corrao standing above him, rifle in hand. The barrel of his gun, they thought, still warm.

This is where all the stories come from. There are some, even now, who will say it was Corrao who brought him down. The tongues, the wagging tongues of Palermo, they whispered and whispered for years, about Corrao and his jealous heart. Corrao, the man who would be general, as if there was need for a general.

And these same nasty, lying tongues are the same who say it was Corrao who shot Rosalino Pilo, up in the hills above Monreale. The same jealous heart, from the street urchin of Alberghia who passed himself off as Doctor Calogero, that lying heart wanted to beat in the chest of a high and powerful General. Corrao was such a one as could not be trusted, because his desire and hunger was so deep in him it was murderous, when he was given a chance. Both times, in the heat of battle, given the opportunity, Corrao could not resist his own murderous envy. It was in his soul, deep in his soul.

"This is what they say, Naguine," Burton told her. "But it is only their disappointment talking, my Little One. It was only their own murderous envy talking."

You see, Rob, Jack Burton was there. He was at both places, he knows what happened at the Monastero, and at Aspromonte. Burton was there, and he can still tell the tale, to set things right, Rob.

Jack Burton was quiet then, sitting and staring at the rumpled sheets on Naguine's bed. She told him, this is why you are running, because of this lie. But he shook his head no.

"Surely some would prefer that I was dead and gone," Burton said, "and then they could tell their tales the way they want them told. But it is not these people who want my head."

Burton laughed at the end of his story then, but he would say little more to Naguine that night. Nothing more than a repeated, "I was there." And once, out of nowhere, on the verge of his sleep, he whispered, "It was my shot.

I went searching in a record store in downtown Jesi, and when that was a dead end, I drove into Ancona and went there to the University library. With everything in Italian it was tough, but it was a day by the sea away from the long shadow of Jack Burton's overflowing stories. It was, though, not a day away from Naguine.

You see, my dear brother, her liquid brown eyes have begun to burn their way into my heart, and I'm not sure now, Rob, if I'm still searching for Burton. When Naguine sits besides me, and I long to kiss her pointed, pretty chin, I realize that it is not me she is interested in. With a pain as sharp as a stab wound, I know this is true. She tells me her stories about Jack Burton in order to hold her dear Burtoni close. He has taken over her soul in the same way she has taken in mine. And I listen to her, no longer in search of Burton, Rob, but in order to listen to her voice and too look into her eyes. Burton's crazy stories are gone for me, brother, though I know that is almost sacrilege to say this to you. But it is Naguine I need to know more about, and I search for her now in all the little comments and memories tossed in among the yarns and adventures of Burton.

I keep her talking about Burtoni so that I don't have a reason to go away.

So it was I went to Ancona to find out about Naguine. I went to find out who this husband of hers was, for maybe, when we've exhausted Jack Burton in her life, maybe this musician in her past will give me some reason to stay behind, a reason to sit beside her longer, perhaps for nights on end.

Still Naguine speaks of him only with extreme care, never with a name, always beside some other topic, just faint hints of him on the periphery of her life. She is protecting him, I know, because of some belief in his spirit and its need to rest.

So in Jesi and then in Ancona, I try to search him out, this guitarist with an illustrious past, yet without a name. And in the library I collect a list of famous guitarists. Especially the obscure guitarists. But the greatest players on the continent in the time between the wars, some of them with names that will live forever, like Django and his brother Nin-nin, but there are many of them who never recorded, or left few recordings, like Baro Ferret and Auguste Malha and Oscar Aleman. And others, already forgotten and left to footnotes of arcane reference books and odd inaccurate histories of lost music: The Brothers Garcia, Coco and Matteo and Serrani, or perhaps Poulette Castro. All of them just names left behind in books, listed in silent indexes, with no sound left to be heard.

One of these men, perhaps, is the unnamed husband of Naguine, or Sophia, if that is her true name. Perhaps she is the widow of the great Django, or of Oscar Aleman. But perhaps it was someone else, someone whose name and music is forever lost to the world, gone like the breath of a flower, vanished in the spring breezes left only to the dying memory of a few, only fleeting briefly across a scattering of old and lost minds.

I generated the longest list I could, in that afternoon in the library, and heard in my mind only the strains of all those guitars, like the ashes left behind in their dead fire. It became a reverie, sitting alone in a library carrel, listening in my mind to this music that I hoped had filled the memories of Naguine. Naguine.

"Serrani," she said, looking past me at the dark evening sky. Her brown eyes saw what couldn't be seen. "Serrani. I'd forgotten him," and this brought a smile to her lips, and it wrinkled the sweet point of her chin. "Yes, he could play," she said, then she looked at me, with one eyebrow raised archly. "He was beautiful, too. Serrani. Matteo and Coco were good, but we girls we liked to gaze at Serrani while he played. His little black mustache, and his black, black eyes. And always that Galousies dangling from his lips. Oh, yes, we liked to watch him play."

The names, I thought. So these men were off the list. She spoke their names, and so they were not him, not the musician without a name.

"Problem was," she laughed at her memory, "Serrani knew we all liked to look at him. And that made him dangerous."

Naguine laughed again and hugged me then, delighting in the memory of old nights when she was a girl, and Serrani was a danger, more than she could handle. He would not be a problem now, I thought. The smile on her lips as she held me, the way she cocked her head back when she laughed, I think they could fill me for days on end. I did hug her back, and she lingered a little too long in my embrace for it to be accidental. She was becoming the dangerous one now. At least for me.

When she let go of me, and eased away, I tried to remember the names on my list, but they were all gone. All of them. I could only recall the most famous one of all, the unforgettable one, the maestro. So I said, "Did you hear Django play?"

Naguine looked at me, and her pretty eyes wrinkled almost closed. She pulled away and gazed distantly at me, and then she reached over and touched my cheek with her warm fingertips.

"Why do you want to know all these things?" she said. "All these things about me?" She laughed a bit at that and her fingertips moved down along my cheek until she touched my neck, and played with the collar of my shirt. "I thought you were here to find Signor Burtoni."

I admit it, Rob, I was struck. The warmth of her touch had confused me, and I had nothing more to say. Nothing. And so she went on then, with Jack Burton's story. But it was not because I was pursuing him, not because I had asked her to tell me more. It was because she wanted to continue his story, wanted to conjure him back between us. So we know the rest of this story, Rob, despite me, not because I pursued it in any way. Not past this point.

"'They hauled him down to the port at Scilla,' Burtoni told me." Naguine kept an arm around my waist as she spoke. I felt her warmth. We were inside her wagon, sitting side by side, on the edge of her bed.

"They carried Burton?" I asked, thinking we knew at last something of how he was injured.

"No, the General," Naguine said. "Il Generale's ankle had been shattered by that shot from Burtoni's gun, or from some stray shot, I guess."

He was, as the General always was, fearless and strong. He could no longer stand, and he told the doctors to amputate immediately if they needed to cut at all. But they refused, and after the surrender at Aspromonte, Pallavicino had him carried down in a litter to a ship in the harbor at Scilla.

"I remember it clearly," Burton said to Naguine, and then he pulled himself up straight in his chair as he spoke about it for a long while.

They carried him on board the Duca Di Genova, and from on her decks the Generale pulled himself up onto his feet again and saluted to Cialdini, that bastard. One soldier to another. One the conqueror and creator of Italia, now a prisoner of the country he'd made. The other a little lap dog of the King, a marcher in the courtyard and never on a battlefield. And then Cialdini, the little son of a bitch, he refused to return the General's salute.

"'When Corrao and Burton saw that they realized the royalist generals could not be trusted. They recognized it right away. Right from that moment on the shore at Scilla, they understood it all.

You see, Pallavicino had made promises, when the General surrendered. There were many, many promises made at that surrender. But the General wanted only one thing: amnesty, complete and total for all his army. Amnesty for the Thousand, and especially for those like Matteo who had deserted from the King's army to join the Thousand in their crusade for Rome. Burton and Corrao held him up between them, and his son Menotti rushed to his side, before the General fell onto the litter that carried him down to Scilla and to the prison ships. But before he fell into the King's hands, he addressed us all, leaning then on Menotti's shoulder.

"Lay down your arms, my heroes," the Generale said. "You will not be forgotten by me, O my men, nor punished by your new country for trying to free our capitol, the capitol of our destiny." And so, as they always did, the Red Shirts trusted in his words and followed him as best they could. They all surrendered, and marched in loose order down through the foothills into Scilla. Corrao and Burton, with Matteo along, they followed the General's litter down.

But Giovanni Corrao always kept about him the wits of Dottore Calogero. So at Corrao's lead, they began to fall back to the rear, he and Matteo and Burton. The rest of the Red Shirts, the Thousand and more, they pressed forward to stay close to their wounded General, to follow his litter toward the ships. And ringed around them all were the soldiers of Vittorio Emanuele, the battalions of Pallavicino.

But like a cat with an instinct to stay wild, Corrao held the three of them back to the rear. And then they saw the salute. They saw that pompous ass in a uniform, they saw him turn away and refuse to salute their General.

"See," Corrao said to Burton, "I told you." And so off came his red shirt, and with just a nod of the head from him, Matteo and Burton did the same. At that moment, there was a great "Huzzah!" that rose up from the Thousand and more. The General had saluted his men from the decks of the Duca di Genova, and the whole crowd pressed forward.

And Corrao used the pandemonium of that moment, when the Red Shirts pressed forward toward the ship and Cialdini's army reacted at once with fear. Would that unarmed mass of fiery red swarm onto the Duca di Genova? Swarm over the guns of the King? Their bayonets flashed, and little Pallavicino shouted orders no one could hear.

With just a glance at us, Corrao led Matteo and Burton away. They were bareback now and sweating in the August sun of the Mezzogiorno, and no one seemed to notice as the three quietly slipped away and joined the crowd of onlookers. They became peasants, fieldworkers from the hills, anyone but a soldier of the Thousand.

Burton dropped his red shirt on the ground alongside Corrao's, and later they pilfered a little laundry from a window on their way out of Scilla on foot. But even before that, bareback and sweaty, they looked only like poor Calabrian laborers.

So they stole a little fishing boat, sky blue and lined with strong red edge, and they rowed again across the Strait to Messina. "Where are we going?" Matteo asked once they were out of sight of the lights of Messina. It was only then that Burton noticed what Matteo had done.'

"Palermo," shouted Corrao, "We can hide in Palermo as long as we want."

"Or as long as we need to," Burton answered him.

But that little Matteo, he had with him still, stuck under his arm now, the red shirt the General had given him. He was still carrying it.

"Get rid of it," Corrao told him.

"Never. Not as long as I live."

"Lad, that shirt will be the death of you," ordered Corrao. "I'll get you another one when we reach the Albergheria."

"Never," said Matteo again.

And so there was no point in arguing anymore. In Messina they put their trust in no one, not even their old comrades from their days with Pilo. Not any of them. And Burton fell silent in telling his story, refusing to name any names, as if he was all these years later still protecting some rebels or insurgents. "It was only later," Naguine said to me, and now she glanced away. "I realized it was her. He didn't want to mention her name to me."

"Rafaella Crisiana," I said.

Naguine looked back at me, and her brown black eyes were watery and filled with sadness. She didn't say the name either, but I could see the hurt. All this time, all these years passing, and Burton's love for that woman in Sicily would neither die, nor even grow cold. Not even with her grave between them. And I could see then the pain in Naguine's eyes. Her Burtoni, her last love, perhaps her only love, could never truly love her, he could never give his heart entirely away, for the main part of it always and forever belonged only to "her," to Rafaella in her dusty grave.

It was then, Rob, without a pause, that I reached over and pulled Naguine to me. Her waist was soft and easy, and she came gently into my arms. I meant at first, I think, only to console her, for I felt for her pain, and I felt the long, old pain of Jack Burton too. My gesture was meant to be only an embrace, a consolation. But then, somehow, in some totally unplanned way, our lips met and we kissed.

I think that Naguine, in her heart, was still giving herself over to Burton. It was not me, truly, that she kissed. But at that moment, to me it did not matter.

Because that night everything changed, Rob. I could never go back to where I was, to what I had become. In that long and sudden kiss, my life changed course. The days of grad schools and academic careers, of safety in the groves of the academy melted away, and a different future emerged for me, little brother. I have become a wanderer, Rob. My home, as it is for Naguine, as it is for the great Burtoni himself, it is nowhere. Like a chain of causation, except that of course there is no cause or effect involved, the kiss of Rafaella Crisiana unmoored forever the ancient soul of Jack Burton. And for Naguine, it was Burton's kiss that led her away from the caravan's of her people, and made her a solitary. I know that to her tribe, to her family, his touch, his kiss, his embrace made her unclean, as he was unclean. It made her, at once, powerlessly alone and filled her with the endless power of independence. And when she kissed me, that night, it freed my gypsy soul too. The soul I didn't even know I had.

I know, you are saying to yourself in the midst of this long letter that is supposed to be about Jack Burton, that she is at least twenty years older than I am. Probably more. But I think I'm trying to tell you, Rob, that in searching for that great wanderer Jack Burton of the Red Shirt, Il Rosso of the Thousand, I'm trying to tell you, Rob, I think I have become Jack Burton.

In the morning, we awoke in her trailer, with the covers over us to keep out the morning cold, warm in the warmth of our two bodies. There was no remorse, there was no bashfulness, but instead there was a new closeness, as we shared our nearness to one another, and to the spirit of Burtoni that lingered over us both.

Later in the day, after we had eaten, Naguine sighed distractedly and she muttered, "Poor Matteo. He was as young as you are."

"What do you mean?" I said.

"That boy was executed, you know," Naguine said. Her eyes rested on me, and I believe she might be seeing that young Matteo in me. "They took the Generale and his son and half a dozen more of them off to prison in the North, in Liguria. And Burtoni and Corrao worked their way cautiously across Sicily to
Palermo. After a few months, the General was released and allowed to go home to Caprera. But Matteo, he didn't make it to home, or Palermo. He didn't make it anywhere."

"Why?" I said.

"Because he was young, he was still a dreamer," Naguine reached across the table where we sat over black coffee and a few blood red oranges, and she took my hand in hers gently. "He was still an idealist, like you are." She ran her index finger, with its bright red nail, softly across the heel of my palm.

"But what happened to him?"

"Burtoni told it, he said that Matteo just didn't believe anything he'd done was a crime. He was a patriot, he thought. Mostly he was young."

"He was a patriot," I said.

"Yes, he was," Naguine stroked the back of my hand softly then. "But he was also a deserter from the Royal Army, and the leader he followed was in prison for treason. It was then he decided to turn himself in. The young boy turned himself in."

"He did what?"

"That's right. Burtoni and Corrao tried to stop him. They were, the three of them, working their way on foot to Palermo. And they were 'borrowing' a few boats along the northern coast, too. When they were near Spadafora, Matteo up and announced to Burtoni that he was going to turn himself in. He would report in at Milazzo, just ahead. He was not a deserter, he was a hero, Matteo insisted. 'But don't let Giovanni know,' Matteo said.

"So, of course, that's just what Burtoni did. He went straight to Giovanni Corrao and told him what Matteo planned.

"'Stupid kid,' Corrao shouted. 'They'll toss him in jail on some island and throw the keys into the ocean.' If only that was the case. But there was no stopping Matteo, Burtoni told me. He was already gone, in truth.

"'I'm not guilty of anything,' the kid had said. He put on his red shirt again and walked off then, headed back alone for Messina instead of Milazzo, and no one ever saw him again."

"He just disappeared?" I said.

Naguine wrapped her hands around mine as if we were praying together, and pressed them to her chest as if I was a lost child found. "You could say that," she whispered in my ear.

"What happened to him?" I demanded, but I didn't pull my head away from her embrace.

"No one knows for sure," Naguine went on, and gradually her embrace of my hands went slack. "You see, my dreamer, there was around Messina then, in those days right after Aspromonte, when the Generale was locked up in a prison ship still, headed North, there was Major in the Royal Army. His name was Dell'Utri. Silvio Dell'Utri. This Major Dell'Utri in those days before the amnesty came and the Thousand were all freed, before that he rounded up a handful, maybe a dozen or so, of the soldiers who had deserted from the Royal Army to follow Il Generale. Dell'Utri put them up against a church wall, and shot them all dead before a firing squad. Then Major Dell'Utri and his men stripped the bodies clean, and burned their clothing in a red, tall bonfire, while he buried every one of them naked in one mass grave."

"And Matteo?" I said.

Naguine paused, and though neither of us knew this poor boy from the past, it was a long silence. "Burtoni believes Matteo wound up in that unmarked grave, with a dozen others. But he was never seen again. Never."

Naguine took a long sip from her coffee then. I split open a rosy orange with my thumb and peeled it away some, and the dark red juice spilled onto my fingers.

"You know what is even worse? Burtoni said it was the worst that could happen, after that." Naguine looked at the red juice on my hands, watched as I tasted its bitterness with my tongue. "That Major, that man Silvio Dell'Utri, he got away with it. The government in Torino didn't want any more trouble, and people from all over Europe were calling for the General to be freed. So Il Generale was released and went home to recover on his island. And everyone just wanted it all to be over. So the grave was never found, and Major Dell'Utri slipped away to the North. And the whole world just looked the other way."

She took my hand again, and kissed away the sticky juice. I fed her an orange pip red as my blood, and we stopped talking, of Matteo, of Major Dell'Utri, of Burtoni, for a while.

So I know from what Naguine told me, and I think too from things Old Sister Teresa said in Siracusa, and maybe, Rob, from things Burton said that night years and years ago when we were just boys, enchanted in his firelight, I know that he went to live in Palermo. He and Giovanni Corrao lived in the Albergheria quietly for a year. I suppose they took on assumed names. I'm sure they did. Corrao became Dottore Calogero again, I imagine, and he treated the mad and the sick with his hands and his potions, and probably most of all with the smoke from that blackened sweet powder of his. I don't know what Burton called himself, but I suppose there may have been many names. It doesn't matter. It was a dark year of silence and mystery, when Jack Burton labored on fishing boats and on the docks to earn a few lire to live. He and Corrao, or Calogero, tucked themselves away in an alley somewhere, and they just pretended not to exist.

Tonight we are sitting outside, by a blazing fire, under the shadowy hills lined with row upon row of vines filled with verdicchio grapes. I have an arm around Naguine, around her soft, full waist, and I hold her to me. Her body keeps me warmer than the fire. Still she is distant, though I hold her tight. She is in the arms of her Burtoni, I suppose. For earlier, after the sun had long set, when I rose to stack wood on the fire against the damp and cold of the oncoming night, Naguine drew her little box and her pipe from somewhere in the multi-colored blouse she wore, and she lit up two tiny bowls of it, but not for me. Perhaps one of them was for the Burtoni who sat with her in her mind. In just a few, deep swallowed breaths, the black paste was gone, with little or no trace of its scent even in the air. She took them both, without even a glance at me. There was not even a gesture toward sharing it.

We'd had wine, and perhaps I had breathed in a little of her smoke in the air, but before long she lay against me, and her eyes, her wonderful black eyes deep as the Adriatic, were just slits of sleepy shadows, and her head then rested on my shoulder, and all that magical black hair of hers fell around my shoulders and surrounded me.

In that strange, helpless stillness, she began to talk. "He only mentioned her to me once," Naguine said. I didn't

49

say a word, under her spell where I stayed, but I knew she meant Rafaella, the one great love of Jack Burton's long life. "Only once did he talk about her," Naguine said, and I answered with my silence in the faint diminishing night. Naguine filled that night with her voice, telling the story Burton told.

"'That was how they knew,' Burton had said to Naguine and then he hung his head low as he spoke, too. He was filled with deep sadness again. 'I was the one who gave us up to the knives, and those short, bitter blades were meant for me, my Little One. They were meant for me. Not for Giovanni.'

For some foolish reason, Burton got the idea in his head--it was just vain, stupid hope—but he thought if he could just find Rafaella, he could tell her what had happened, and she would understand, then. She would know how her father died that day, and most of all, Burton believed she would forgive him. So he went up to Monreale, where they had made their vows to one another that night long before. He went up there on the same night, only two years later. On their anniversary, I guess I should call it. It made no sense, but he believed he would find her there, because it was the anniversary, the night, they pledged their eternal love to one another, the night they were married in their hearts. So he went back to where they had promised to love and trust one another forever, believing somehow

50

she would be there, and believing that promises would hold true.

Burton went to mass there, under those glorious mosaics, and in the evening candlelight the hand of the Lord reached out and engulfed everything and everyone, and he was filled with his desperate hopes. Afterwards, he walked back in the moonlight into the cloister, and she was there.

Burton said to her, "Rafaella," and he walked toward her. He was about to say more, to begin to try to explain how everything between them had come apart, to explain the death of her father, and what had happened that day at Castellnotte. But before he could approach she glanced up, and it was immediately clear that she had not come there expecting to find him. "You," was all she said. She didn't say his name, just that one word of shock and surprise. "You."

And then Burton saw that she wasn't alone. Beside her, wrapped in the flowing folds of her skirt to keep the child warm, was a little girl.

Jack Burton bent down on his knees, to be closer to the child, but Rafaella drew the little girl away from him, deeper into her skirts, and the girl, who was fair and rosy white as her mother, was sleepy and bashful, reading instinctively her mother's fears, the little girl hid her face shyly in her two tiny hands.

"Where are you?" Rafaella said. She didn't ask what he was doing there, near the Cloister of Monreale. It was obvious to them both why he was there, but Rafaella didn't want to talk about that.

So Burton told her then about Corrao, and how they were living in the Albergheria., about their jobs and their shifting names, and then he started to try to explain again how her father had died. He managed to say only the first word of it. He said, "Castellnotte.'"

51

But that was all. Rafaella held up her hand as if toward off a demon, and it stopped him. She didn't want to hear it, not one word of it. For her there was no explaining. It was all too painfully clear. She picked up the little girl and held her away from him, shielding the child with her body, and then she said goodbye.

As she started to walk away, he stopped her by asking, "What's her name?" At first Rafaella didn't respond, and just continued to walk away with her back to him. "What is our daughter's name?" Burton shouted in that vast space beneath the mosaics, with the Creator looking down on us. For he knew, from the moment he saw the child, she was theirs.

Rafaella turned around once, and now she had her hand over the back of the child's head, pressing his daughter's face deep into the fold of her blouse. "She's not yours," Rafaella said flatly.

"What's her name?" he repeated stubbornly.

"Rosalina," she answered, softly, as if not to wake the child. But the girl was wide-awake, squirming to get free, maybe wanting just too look up at Burton, this stranger who upset her mother. Then Rafaella turned again and walked away, out of the church, out of Monreale. Out of the rest of Burton's life. He never saw Rafaella again. Never again.

But he knew only one thing for sure. Rafaella wanted him to believe that this child was the daughter of Rosalina Pilo. She wanted Burton to believe that she and Pilo were lovers. But she had forgotten one thing herself. Burton knew Rosalino Pilo, and loved him like an older brother. Burton was there when Pilo died at San Martino; Burton saw the shot that killed him in his prime, before Rosalino could see the march of the Thousand into his old Palermo. He knew him. And he knew Rafaella, too. It was her father Lombardo who had worn many faces, not Rafaella. And not Pilo.

Naguine said to me, "That child, Rosalina Crisiana, she was his daughter.'

That was when I reached up, Rob, and touched Naguine's cheek with the tips of my fingers. I swept the long black hair back away from her face, and I kissed her on the forehead. I didn't say anything, because I didn't know anything to say. But I could no more comfort her than she could comfort Jack Burton. There was no comfort to be had. Not for any of us, Rob. Not then. And not now.

After a while, Naguine spoke without lifting her head from my shoulder. "Burtoni kept saying to me all that night, 'They wanted me, and I gave him up.' All through that night, he said not a word more about that woman or about his child. Not one more word. I gave him everything I had to give that night. And he took it, my darling Burtoni took it all. But it didn't matter, because still he said, over and over, whenever the night was silent and calm, aloud he spoke and in a whisper too, 'They wanted me, and I gave him up.'"

"He gave up Corrao," I said. Naguine didn't answer at all, but that only meant I understood completely.

*   *   *

Now comes the craziest part, or at least that is what you will think, Rob. I guess even to me, it seems mad. But it didn't seem that way that night, not in any of those days I spent with her. And if things were different, even now, I would do it all again. And maybe the end result would be different. Maybe.

I think, Rob, I'm writing all this to you now to try again to explain it myself. I started out, you know, to report to you what I found here. But now, now it is all different. And I need to know how, even if I can't know why.

It was just a few days later, Naguine and I were strolling along the Esino, enjoying the spring sun blazing on the stream and on the vineyards lining the brown hills above us. The sky was almost a silver blue, and the rows of verdicchio vines were just beginning to show off their budding leaves, while the Esino was running high, full of snow melt and all the signs of life reborn. I was holding her hand, and we were lazy as children without a care or worry, and I proposed to her then.

"This has become my home," I said to her. She smiled but didn't respond. I suppose she thought I meant this valley outside of Jesi, so I tried again. "I don't mean here, in Jesi, Naguine. I meant you."

She stopped walking, but didn't let go of my hand. Her dark eyes were smiling, and she lowered her head a bit, and cocked it to the side, so her long black hair fell over the tip of her shoulder.

"You have become my home," I said, finally.

The silence of her response was unnerving. Though her eyes were filled with fondness, she said nothing. After a few minutes of, for me, endless and nervous quiet, I began to walk along the riverbank again. I was still holding her hand, but it was more like clinging now. So I wove my yarn out into the springtime air, like a fine fabric of dreams spread under that silver blue sky, the way I understood it all. It was intoxicating, as if the vines of verdicchio had filled the air with their sweet, dry liquor. I would become a traveler I said, just like she was, along with her. We would be our own band of gypsies, following the summer sun north into Europe, and letting it lead us with its warmth south in the winter. Free, attached only to one another, we would live easily, wandering from market to bazaar, plying our little trade to get along. But always and everyday, we would be together.

I'm afraid I went on for a long while, sounding more desperate the longer I talked. And realizing as I talked that, unlike her, I had no trade to ply. Still her silence was the answer I didn't want to hear, and so I talked and talked and talked, because if I paused she would have time to tell me that I belonged somewhere else, back with my schools and colleges, back in my dry and barren studies. Oh, it seemed so frigid then, in the warming light of Le Marche along the banks of the slow, full Esino. But eventually, I ran out of words to say. And still, she had not answered the question I was afraid to ask.

*   *   *

Instead of answering, Naguine told me her story. She stopped walking and sat us both down on a large stone by the water, warmed by the easy afternoon sun.

"My husband was only ill for a little while," she said, holding my hand in her two hands in her lap. "I was still very young, younger even than you, and so I didn't see any signs of it coming at us. We were up above the Padna, near the foot of the Alps, just enjoying the early spring coming on, like it is today here. He even spoke about how we needed to move over to Nizza soon, where he could play and make some money before we traveled back up to Paris for the summer season.

"That afternoon, he just went for a stroll alone, like he often did, to have a smoke beside a creek there, under a tree somewhere. But he came back to the wagon too soon, not having been gone for even an hour. He said he was feeling dizzy, and his forehead was warm from a fever. So he went to bed inside the trailer, at the height of day. It only seemed like a cold coming on. That was all. How could I know?

"In the morning, he didn't get out of bed. He just lay there, not sleeping, but just lying around. In the afternoon, I got him to sit up and eat, and he said he felt better, that maybe he wouldn't catch the cold after all. He asked for his guitar and all the rest of the daylight he played, fast, dancing runs on the strings, he played boleros and czardas, and 'Nuage' and 'Honeysuckle Rose' and 'Blue Drag.' He played alone like that until darkness fell, and then he set his guitar aside. He told me how he'd learned on a six-string banjo when he was a kid, because a guitar was too quiet to be heard in a band, it was only good for rhythm. No one could hear your melodies over the violins and the accordion and the horns. He patted his guitar, it was big as a cello and made of smooth blonde wood, and he told me what I already new, that he'd had this guitar specially made, that is why it was so big, so it was loud enough to be heard, but still sang with the warmth of the wood, and not the bright slap of the skin on a banjo.

"I believe he knew what was happening, and he was saying goodbye to me, and to his music. I began worry him then, about getting him to a doctor, to see what was wrong. He never, never believed in doctors, and he always fought about even going near them. So I should have been suspicious then, about how bad he was feeling, because he agreed with me. Right away, without any arguing. He said in the morning, if he didn't feel any better, we would go to find a doctor in Verona. I should have known right then what he was about. But I was still so young and trusting. What did I know?

"The next morning, of course, he never woke up. By the time the sun rose, he was gone, warm still to my kisses, but gone. We took him in the afternoon to a church near there, and the priest gave him a mass, and there were just all of us in the family then, Gyorgy and Aziz and Giuseppe and their wives, Elena, Emilia and Sofia. And me. That evening we buried him there in the churchyard at Asolo, and then we all went back out to our camp in the countryside. Everyone, the priest especially, was happy to see us go. They wanted it all over fast, and that was fine. It was our way.

"But the next day, that was the time that was truly amazing, Will. That was when I realized how special he was. For us he was dead and buried, and it was time for his spirit to move on, and be free of attachments to us. We never again spoke his name. Never once have I spoken it. But even despite that, among the musicians the word of his death spread with the winds and the breezes. Some of the musicians began to turn up late on the day we buried him, and by noon the next day there was a crowd in our camp. They came from all over, from other camps of the people, you know. But mostly they were gadje. A lot of them came on trains, and some in their motorcars. The famous one's like the violinists Stephane and Stuff who loved him, they came in the long, black motorcars with drivers.

"The Garcia brothers pulled up together in a big Packard, Coco and Matteo with Serrani too in the back seat, with a little gray in his moustache but still turning all the girls' heads. Baro Ferret was there, and August Malha, way up in his eighties then and not long for the world himself, but he came. Poulette Castro and Oscar Aleman came driving down from Paris, together in a swift little Bugati two-seater. The Bugati belonged to Poulette, Oscar told me, a little touch of sad envy in his voice. Not long after them on a little Gilera motorbike, Nin-nin rode in, bringing his apologies. His brother was away in the studios back in Paris, making records with some of the men who played with the Duke, and so he couldn't get away. He couldn't come."

Naguine pressed my hand a little tighter, and looked over my head at the hillsides, and said, "After dark, once we'd started the fire, Burtoni arrived. I don't know from where. He embraced me, and his eyes were red from the tears. How he knew, how they all knew so quickly, it was like magic. As if something was in their bloodstream, they all knew that part of the music had died."

Naguine let go of my hand and she folded her hands together at her waist, and she was about to stand up. But I covered her folded hands with mine, and she stayed sitting beside me. "The music they played that day. It was something. Because you know, it was simple. They were all, every one of them, masters. Virtuosi. But that day, and probably that day alone, there was no showing off. There was no competition. At least, they didn't compete with flourishes and speed. No, it was all simple. And if they competed, it was to see who could put the deepest feeling into every note.

"So they played the afternoon sun away, with hardly a pause, and precious few words, just strains and strains of endless melody, running toward the dark. As the evening came on, we began to build the fire, and the family helped me as we hauled out all of his things, and put them on the pyre. We needed to free his soul from us, from his brothers and sisters and friends, and from me. And even from the musicians, too. So everything he owned, everything that was his, it all went into the flames.

"The last thing of all was the most precious. When the fire was burning at its highest, I brought out his great blonde guitar, and I hurled it into the flames."

Naguine shook her head and laughed then, and hugged herself. There was a fretful frown on her lips that wrinkled up her pretty chin. "It was Burtoni who couldn't take it," she said through her laugh. "But then he wasn't one of us, so he didn't understand. He may be an old soul and a wise one too, but he is still gadjo, so he didn't understand." She paused a moment, and then looked straight into my eyes as if to warn me of these truths. "It's why I am alone. Why I travel by myself now," she said. And those words pierced my heart.

I couldn't ask her more then, for fear of what I'd learn. I realize now I didn't want to understand what she meant. Though I did understand, right at that moment, I didn't want to. So instead I asked about Jack Burton, and not about Naguine.

"What did Burton do?" I said.

"He pulled the guitar from the fire, and held it in his lap. 'We must save this,' he called out to everyone and to

59

no one, and he held that great instrument up before us. 'It was his,' Burtoni said. 'So we can remember him.'"

I knew that Burton must have spoken his name at that point, though Naguine even now carefully left it out.

"It was Nin-nin who took it away from Burtoni," Naguine went on proudly, that wrinkled frown turning to a wistful smile. "Nin-nin took the guitar in his hands, and announced to us all, 'Django could not be here, but instead he told me to bring you this.' And then Nin-nin began to play Django's old tune 'Nocturne' for him, and slowly everyone else joined in."

"Django's 'Nocturne' was composed for your husband?" I said.

"On that day, as everyone played it, it was," Naguine nodded her head as she spoke, as if in the slow rhythm of the song.

"When they were finished, Nin-nin took the guitar and he handed it to me, knowing what I would do. He explained to Burtoni, 'We must let his spirit go, my friend. It is our way," he said, as I put the great blonde guitar back onto the pyre, and slowly it went up in flames. For a long while, as that instrument burned, we were all silent. But when the neck cracked in two from the force of the steel strings on the steel struts, Matteo and Serrani began to play again, and before long everyone joined in. And then the music flowed and flowed all night, until the dawn sent us, one at a time, away to sleep it off by the cooling ashes of the fire."

*   *   *

That was how she said no to me, Rob. I never asked her again. I never tried to object, or to plead my love. Though I wanted, no, that's not right. I still want to ask why, to plead yes, to whisper why not to her. But it has never once come up again between us. Never.

"I kept saying to Burtoni," Naguine told me, a few days later, "it was Aspromonte. It was all revenge for what happened at Aspromonte. That was why Giovanni Corrao died. You know, many people still blame him for that gunshot that felled the General. Many, many of them did."

A week or two had gone by, and I knew now that I would have to leave eventually. But I was searching for ways to stall it off, and Jack Burton's story, Rob, has become my only reason not to say farewell to Naguine. So now, I pursue it like a last thread of hope.

Naguine and I spent days and days as the summer came on, and the iris began to bloom in the gardens of Jesi, and I lingered. I was living with her then, and I know that the time had come and gone for her to move on, to the next market, to deliver the clothes she had mended, to take in more work to be done. I know that Naguine missed several of her appointed rounds then, and I took that in my stupidity as a faint ray of hope. There would be grumbling from her

61

customers later. But still she lingered with me, and my silly dreams allowed me to fool myself.

But for her it was all about Jack Burton. Talking to me, telling his story, kept Burton alive for her. And so my presence gave her a reason to talk about him. And for me, Burton's story gave me a reason to linger in Naguine's embrace, and to bask in her deflected attentions.

I was sitting on the floor of the trailer, leaning against the bed where Naguine sat, sewing by hand as she altered someone's shirt. She wore a long, brown skirt that reached nearly to the floor, and her feet were bare. Her toenails were painted a red that was nearly as dark and brown as her eyes. My hand was wrapped around her ankle, holding her in that way in the warmth of late afternoon.

"'No,' Burtoni would say to me," Naguine's dark eyes were lowered, as she concentrated on the needle moving deftly in her hands. "'It was me they were after,' he would say, and I couldn't change his mind. He was sure of it. And sure they were still hunting him, too.

"Often he would say, 'Thirteen men died that night in Palermo, including my old comrade, Giovanni Corrao. But it was all for me. All of it. They were searching for me,' he would say. 'They thought they'd found me.'"

"Thirteen men?" I said to Naguine.

She nodded her head, without even glancing up from her needle and thread. "It's still called the Night of Thirteen Daggers, down in Sicily, in Palermo." The point of her chin made the moon shape of her face against her black hair a swift, smooth blade piercing into my heart, as I looked up at her. I embraced her ankle gently in my hand. "You don't know about the Thirteen Daggers?" she never even glanced up from her work, but she kept her foot exposed to my touch.

I said that I hadn't.

With wrinkled concentration furrowing her brow, she worked the fabric around in her hand for a moment, and then she said, still without ever looking at me, "Let me tell it to you the way Burtoni tells it." Though it took her a day or two to tell it all, in the end I pieced it together like this:

The first time that he saw them, he was working as a porter at the train station, at Centrale, Burton told Naguine. He was toting luggage around on a big wooden cart. They were short and dark, and wearing suits that looked like they'd been fitted on them over their peasant clothes, just so they could go to town, and there were three of them. Round heads and black hair oiled back tight, and all of them well short of five feet. With their size and the dark sunburn of their skin, Burton knew they came from the interior, from up in the Madonie. Palermo was no more their home than it was his.

He noticed first the way they were hanging around the station, out in Piazza Cesare, always the three of them together. And no matter who or what Burton carted around, the three of them would turn up somewhere, watching him, but never approaching. Once he nodded to them, but they only glanced away nervously, and acted as if they hadn't seen his gesture.

He'd been around Palermo long enough then to be suspicious of what it meant. So he left work early that day, and he didn't tell anyone where he was going. Burton just abandoned the job, right then and there. He walked slowly up Via Maqueda to the Quattro Canti, without any hurry, and sure enough, those three little men followed him. They tried to hang back, and then they even walked on the other side of Maqueda. But they were following along behind him.

So he turned and went straight into Martorana and strolled up to the front pews right under the lectern, and knelt down there to pray. The church was empty in the late afternoon, except for two old women in black veils whispering to their rosary beads. Burton heard the doors to the church open and close twice behind him, but he didn't turn around to see if it was them.

After enough time had passed so he seemed to have said all his prayers, and was done, he stepped back out of Martorana into the Piazza Pretoria and as he strolled along, there they were, the three of them. They were just sitting around the big fountain in the piazza. So he strolled right past them and nodded again in their direction, to let them know he'd seen them. They still didn't respond, other than to watch Burton saunter by. He headed up toward the Corso. They, of course, followed along at a distance.

It wasn't hard to lose them, though. He just hurried across the bustling Corso, stopping to wave at them from the other side. It was clear they were not from Palermo the way they struggled along the busy street. But he turned off into the Vucciria, disappeared into an alley or two, found his way to the back of a fishmonger's stall where he'd worked a few days now and then in the past. It didn't take even a glance for them in the stall to understand he was trying to disappear. They sent him directly out through a back door.

Burton didn't see anymore of those three little backcountry friends that day. But he knew enough not to head back home toward the Albergheria until nightfall. When he told Corrao about them, later that night, Corrao laughed at him.

"They look like they're from back up in the Madonie," Burton said.

Corrao was stretched out on his bed, with his hands tucked behind his head for a pillow. "Burtoni," he said, "the streets of Palermo are full of little men from the countryside."

"I think they're from Castellnotte," Burton said.

That just made Corrao laugh at him a good, loud guffaw. "When did you become such a coward, my old comrade in arms? You, who stood under the guns at San Martino! Time was, you'd have laughed at them, even if they came from Castellnotte." Corrao had a big, deep laugh, you know, and he rolled it out grandly then, and seemed to enjoy himself at Burton's expense. "Even if they looked like the little cousins of old Lombardo the snake."

He reminded Corrao that no one in that country ever forgets anything, and what they did back there in Castellnotte, even if they were the orders of the General himself, it was all remembered. Every bit of it. Everything that was done. All of it.

"There were no orders from the General,'" Corrao said, and now his laugh had disappeared. "Not for what you did."

"I know," Burton said.

"Time was, Gianni Burtoni, you'd still laugh at them, and not be running scared, not even if they all, every little one of them, looked like our sweet, little Rafaella.'

But Corrao shut up then, and there was no more laughing. And Burton had nothing more to say to him. Corrao knew at once he'd gone too far, mentioning her. He knew how they had been. And Burton had told Giovanni Corrao about how he'd gone back to Monreale that night, and about the child. So Corrao shut up then, and there was no more of his big laughter. He'd gone too far, and he knew it.

They didn't talk about any of it for a week or more, not about Lombardo or Castellnotte and what went on there, and not anymore about the three little men following Jack Burton around downtown Palermo. But a week or so later, Corrao realized that not only had Burton abandoned his porter's job at the Stazione Centrale, he had not even gone back for his pay. That, for Giovanni Corrao, was too much.

"They owe you for a whole week," he said in amazement. "You're so scared, you're just going to let them keep your money?"

Burton told him it wasn't worth that little bit of money, not to let those toughs from the Castellnotte hills find them. And they didn't need the money. He was lying low, just like Corrao should be. That's what Burton told him.

But this was just not the way Giovanni Corrao worked. So he put on his best Dottore Calogero suit and he strutted on up to the office at Centrale, and he demanded all the money. He told them that Burton had gotten sick so he wasn't coming back for a while, but that Burton owed him money for the medicine he'd given him. Even in Stazione Centrale, in the office, they'd heard of Dottore Calogero. So they gave up the pay, or the better part of it, since the manager kept his 'fee' for holding the money. Giovanni didn't get it all, but he got all he was going to get, so Giovanni was satisfied.

Yet as he was leaving the station, Corrao saw their three friends, or probably three more of them, knowing what we all know now. But Corrao, being Giovanni Corrao, he walked across the Piazza Cesare to where they were leaning against a wall at the corner of Via Maqueda. He agreed with Burton, he told him later. There wasn't any doubt in his mind these men came from back up in the Madonie. They had the faces of Castellnotte.

"'Waiting for somebody?' he asked them, using Sicilian and not Italian.

"'Who wants to know?'" the tallest of the three short men answered back in Sicilian. One of the other two pulled out a dagger and calmly started cleaning his nails with its long thin blade, far too long for how he was using it.

Corrao used Burton's name then. He told those men that he was Gianni Burtoni. At the sound of that name, the little man with the long awkward dagger stopped what he was doing, and then examined Corrao's face. I'm sure, I tell you, he was matching Corrao's face to a description in his head.

"We're not looking for anybody,'" the first man said. But this time he spoke in Italian, and Corrao said he wasn't sure the other two men even knew what was being said.

So Corrao stuck with Sicilian, because he wanted to be sure they all understood. 'If you men need anything else, or if you want to find me, ask around for Calogero. Dottore Calogero. He'll know where to find me.' None of them responded. They just looked him over with silent disdain and acted as if they would never care to see him again.

Corrao repeated in Sicilian, 'In case you need to find me, someday.' Then he turned and strode away down Maqueda. One of the three hung back at a distance, and tried to follow Corrao for a while. But Giovanni knew his way through the alleys of the Albergheria as if they were all perfectly square and straight, and not a twisting labyrinth. He lost his follower when he chose to lose him, and he disappeared down into Palermo's backsides.

*   *   *

About three weeks later, or maybe it was a month, but it was in the hottest part of the high summer, Corrao and Burton were sitting under the awning at Café Rosi, looking out at the Grand Teatro across Piazza Maqueda. They were sipping coffee and trying to stay out of the sun, just waiting lazily for the cool of the evening to return. Burton was slouched low in low chair, still stirring sugar into his cup. Corrao had drained his in a gulp.

The waiter came back with our change, and though he wore a neat suit with a crisp clean collar, he was short and dark like the men from Castellnotte. Burton didn't really notice it at first, because unlike the others, his clothes fit him so well. He didn't seem a stranger to his suit, nor to the busy streets of Palermo either. So it startled him, when he spoke Burton's name.

"Signor Burtoni?" he said. But when Burton looked up, he found the waiter was facing not Burton, but Giovanni Corrao.

Without even batting an eye, Corrao smoothly answered him. "How do you know me?"

"The waiter just shook his head no, as if that didn't matter. He set the few coins down on the white tablecloth in front of Corrao. Burton saw the waiter's sidelong glance examine him, to be sure it was safe to speak. Then he straightened up and his eyes searched the Piazza in front of the Teatro, bustling with carriages and people strolling in the shade and vendors of fruit and ice. The waiter never turned his head, or lifted his body. He just stood at attention, and let his eyes search all around him. He stood as if he were waiting for some orders.

But then quietly and quickly, he said, "You should leave here, Signore."

Corrao glanced over at Burton, but still never let on about the confusion of names. "But we've paid up," Corrao protested ingenuously.

"You should leave Palermo, Signore," the waiter said, whispering through his teeth, though he was still standing at attention. "Soon," he said. Then he turned and was gone, disappearing quickly back inside the café.

Corrao, in the way only he can, he laughed boisterously at him. "What do make of that?" he said.

"He looks like he's from the Madonie, too," Burton said, and he wasn't laughing. "But he's clearly not new to Palermo, is he."

"It's true, my friend," Corrao carefully left out his name, Burton noticed. It hadn't occurred to him until that moment that someone else might be listening and watching. "He's a cousin to our old friends in Castellnotte, but he's been here in the city for a long while."

"Maybe we should pay attention," Burton said, then lifted his cup to his lips.

"This is my home," Corrao said, flatly. Without emotion, he was just stating plain facts. "Nobody is chasing me out of my home." But Jack Burton noticed, he still did not use any part of Burton's name.

"Let's get out of here," Burton said, as he set his empty cup down and stood up. But instead Giovanni headed right back inside the café when he got up, so Burton followed behind him. There he found the waiter, standing with his back to them behind the bar. Corrao strode directly over and said, "Thank you, my brother," to him in loud Sicilian. The waiter turned slowly around, saw Corrao standing there, and then glanced franticly around the room for a moment. Without another word, he stepped back into the darkness of a back room behind the bar, out of our sight and everyone else's. And then, just that quickly, he was gone.

"So you see, my Little One," Jack Burton had said to Naguine, "it was not Aspromonte. It was me they were after. And it was because of what we'd done up in Castellnotte. But the fools, they had our names confused. They couldn't tell me from Giovanni," he paused momentarily, then whispered to Naguine, "But they know now, they do."

"Burtoni would not say any more," Naguine said. "He just hung his head low in deep silence. He muttered a few times, with his head down, 'It was me they were after.'" But he was not speaking to Naguine, or to anyone. She almost couldn't make out what he said; perhaps he was speaking only to his own conscience.

Naguine told me then that she tried to distract him with her kisses and embraces, but on that night he was absent from everywhere except from his memories. He was unapproachable. Lost in his anger and his grief, she realized he was still afraid. "It is why he moves around so much, even now," she said to me. "He won't stay in any one place for long, and he won't put down roots anywhere, no matter how old and frail he gets. But I know, he hungers for a place he can't find. A place that I could give him," Naguine said. I held her in my arms as she told me all of this, but she too was absent, alive only to her memories of Jack Burton. "After what he saw, that one night in Palermo, it is why he will not put down roots with anyone, anywhere," she said more to herself than to me. "Even with me, even though I wander around as much as he does."

I admit it, brother, it made me feel angry and lost, too. I held her in my arms, but she was far, far away and yearning after the embrace of Burton, and not for mine. So I said to her, because I couldn't just be angry, because I was desperate for her attention. "He would put down roots, if it could be with his Rafaella," I said. "Or with his daughter Rosalina."

It was meant to be mean hearted. I said it to make her angry, so that her attention would return to me again. And it worked. With an abrupt shrug of her shoulders, she broke free of my embrace. It was a warm summer night then, and we had been sitting by a low fire outside her trailer. But now she wandered away and off into the dark, in the cottonwoods along the riverbank.

"Naguine, wait, my love," I said, as she walked away into the darkness. "I'm sorry," I said. Then she was gone into the trees and brush. I sat alone for a while, and then I followed her down to the riverside.

There was no moon, so the Milky Way that shone above the Esino was the only light. Naguine sat, her long skirts splayed out over some tall, shaggy grass by the stream. "I'm sorry," I said as I approached her. But she didn't respond, she just stared off into the black waters under the starry night sky. I wanted to repeat it a million times, until it surrounded her. Instead I slipped forward and sat next to her on the ground, listening to the rattle of the low water over the rocks.

In her hands she held that little pipe, and next to her I saw the carved box on the ground. She'd already filled the tiny bowl with the sweet black paste, and for the first and the only time she held the pipe out to me, and then lit the bowl. "Draw in gently," she whispered. "Just let it enter you on its own."

It was easy, I swallowed the white smoke and then let it breathe out of me, and it was so sweet and smooth that I never even coughed. Then I watched as she filled the bowl for herself, and smoked from it twice. Afterwards, she spoke, at least partly to herself. "This is the only thing that gives him any peace," she said.

Suddenly she embraced me then, without another word. Though she was small and lean, her arms around my waist seemed to envelope all of me, and her hair in my face was filled with the scent of dry grass and cinnamon.

Naguine made love to me that night, with our clothes spread out all around us on the grass. It was not the first time, but it was the only time when she was fully in control. I lay tangled in her arms, and in the clothing torn off all around us, and I felt the great and complete unity of her being. All the world vanished into her black eyes, and I lived in the universe of her long arms, and swelled with my whole being in the smooth arch of the low of her back. I murmured my love over and over again into her ears, and into the night sky above us. But Naguine said nary a word in return. She simply and almost silently took total possession of my soul that night. I don't know, still, if she has given it back.

When morning began to break faintly, greening in the East, we lay huddled together under our tangled clothes, exhausted and euphoric. Naguine, in whispered tones, told me the rest of Jack Burton's story then, all in one long whirl. I listened, only half aware, dozing in and out, because my senses were still filled with the taste and scent

72

of her body, and I clung to her, as she did to me, for warmth in the cool of the summer dawn, far from the dying ashes of our fire.

Burton told her:

"I saw them everywhere, after that. Everywhere. Corrao, he laughed at me, he made fun of my worries. He scoffed at the way I looked over my shoulder, whenever anyone came toward us from behind. He laughed and laughed at me. But it didn't matter, for everywhere I went in Palermo, there seemed to be a small dark man hanging around, Naguine. Everywhere I went, one of them was lurking around a corner, or leaning against a wall, or perched in a second floor window, watching me.

"Once to try to escape them, I went into an old, ruined church on Via dei Benedettini, San Giovanni degli Eremeti it was called. I wandered up through its broken old walls into the little cloister up on the side of the hill next to it. In the center of that little cloister, under the shade of an ancient cumquat tree, I sat and rested out of the September heat. The place was empty, except for a workman tending to part of the crumbling walls around the garden, and a brother who strolled in, his hood up over his head so I couldn't see his face, his hands around an open prayer book. The brother walked slowly back and forth, in apparent meditation, and both I and the workman ignored him.

"It was peaceful and quiet there, a refuge from the bustling Palermo streets outside the church grounds, and the bent and twisted limbs of the old tree seemed odd and safe. Time passed, and I was so at peace there, I seemed at long last to rest from all my troubles and all my fears. The old grey bark of the tree and its lime green leaves, they spoke to me of persistence and of hope."

Naguine whispered to me then, as I was still tangled up in her arms, and only half aware of the tale I was being told. The drowsiness of peace and contentment kept threatening to wash over me and carry me off. "You see, it is still on his conscience," she said. "He suffers so, for what happened up at Castellnotte. For the way he was forced to destroy the one thing he loved."

I may have lost awareness, then, for the next thing I remember was Naguine again telling me the story of Burton, and again in Jack Burton's words:

"Just when I felt the peace of true solitude," Burton told her, "I noticed the face of the little brother doing his walking prayers. Our eyes met, and then he quickly glanced away, and I knew he was not praying, no, he was watching me. His face had the dark shadowed hue of the men from the Madonie. You see, even there, even in the cool silent cloister, they were watching me. Always watching me. It seemed to me, Naguine, they were everywhere I turned.

"So I got up in a rush, and did the best I could to disappear into the alleyways north in the Capo, and slowly worked my way around again into the markets of the Vucciria. I did not go back to the Albergheria until nightfall, and until I was relatively sure no one was following me, only then did I finally did turn toward home.

"Oh poor Corrao, he just laughed and laughed and laughed some more at me. He especially liked that I was afraid of an old brother praying in a cloister. 'Gianni,' he laughed at me. 'Half of Palermo looks like they came from the hills around her.'

"'I think half of Palermo is watching us,' I answered him.

"But dear Corrao, he just laughed again, and shook his head as if to say I was impossible, hopeless, far beyond all and any repair. But it was late for him to laugh, late though he didn't know it.

"On the afternoon of October first, Corrao came to our apartment in his suit of clothes dressed as a doctor. He said, 'I had a couple of patients today. Burtoni. They were very nice.' He lowered his head and gazed at me from under his raised eyebrows. "They want to see me tonight. But there are two of them. Trust me, my friend. You will like them, Burtoni. And they owe old Dottore Calogero a big, big debt.'

"He described them both to me, and told me their names, but I don't remember now any of that. He took off his jacket and dusted it off, and he polished his shoes with his spit until they shone, and he whistled a tune from Rigoletto, and I remember he made me put on a suit and a clean collar and he even made me oil my hair. I do remember this, he said, 'She could be the one Burtoni to make you forget that girl of yours in the past.' I remember that he carefully didn't use Rafaella's name, but I don't remember what this girl's name was supposed to be.

"Before we left, he said, 'Let me see.' Then he made me turn around in front of him, and he checked my hands to be sure they were clean. He frowned at them, but I said, 'That's as clean as they come.' Corrao chuckled at me, then he put on a feathered cap and looked in the mirror to be sure it was cocked to the side just so. Then he clapped an arm around my shoulder and said, 'Let's go.'

"At the last moment, just as we stepped out of the door, I remembered that I'd forgotten my watch. Back then

75

it was the prettiest thing I owned, and I thought I should wear it. So maybe Corrao was right, maybe this girl whose name I will never remember, maybe she was the one to let me forget. At any rate, I turned back inside to get it, and Giovanni, glancing back at me over his shoulder, he stepped through the doorway and out into the October night. I heard a quick scuffle of feet on stones, and then I heard him fall, and as I turned back I thought at first that he'd tripped on the stairs."

"You know, he didn't utter a sound, there was not a grunt or a groan. And neither did his attackers. No one said a word. It was dead silence. But when I turned around, this is what I found on the dark street outside. Two short men, dressed in black, dark clothes—it was hard to see then in the poor light—they stood outside past the doorstep. Their faces were masked with black scarves, wrapped around their heads like turbans, so all I saw was the black glint of their eyes. And in their hands I saw the dripping glint of their long thin daggers.

"Between them in the street, face down on the stones, lay Giovanni Corrao. I shouted something at the two daggers, I don't remember what. But their black eyes glared at me, and then they were gone, on the run into the dark alleys of the Albergheria.

"I stumbled out to Giovanni, and kneeling beside him on the stones, as I turned him over I heard the life go out of him like an easy breeze, gently sliding away into a quiet grove beside a cool, spring fed stream. I heard it go out of him. Though I knew he was already gone, after all we'd seen together, after the way we'd stood under fire at San Martino and Milazzo, after we'd marched together through the traitorous streets of Napoli, and stood the charge at Capova. After the way he'd steered me across the dead waters of the Tyrrhenian Sea and through the Straits and into the arms of Rafaella and her father. After all of that, he was gone. Just gone.

"I held him in my lap, and I caressed his hair, while his blood poured out onto the dusty stones. I cried and cried out for help. They'd stabbed him twice: once in the back near his spine, and once into his heart, then slashing down into his bowels with one long smooth stroke. This was the work of butchers, not city men who sell meat, but men of the country, contadini who know how to kill and butcher a pig quickly and efficiently and without struggle. I cried out again for help, though it was all too late. My voice echoed up the empty stone alleyways, and then shortly it was followed by the clicking and turning of latches, clicking and turning, clicking and turning, as the doors and shutters all across the Albergheria silently locked away this trouble, kept it away and outside, and they left me alone kneeling in the narrow street, without a soul who'd even seen the murder on their doorsteps."

"In the morning I learned there were twelve more murders that night, thirteen in all, Naguine. All of them happened at almost the same time, every one of the victims died in the same way, with a dagger plunged into his heart, and with a bloody slash opening the bowels. There were no signs or letters or messages left behind to explain it all. There was no threat to this as retribution, as anything but random death in the streets of Palermo. The victims seemed, in all their variety, to be unconnected. They came from different walks of life, they did not know one another. They were unconnected, and seemed to be chosen to die randomly. None of it made, at first, any sense.

"But the Carabinieri found something they couldn't explain. When the murders were plotted out on a map, their pattern made a strange figure on the streets of the city, like a twelve-pointed star radiating out of one central point. The center, Naguine, the heart of this bloody 12 pointed star, was our doorstep, where Giovanni Corrao, one of the Thousand, the hero of Milazzo, a warrior at the barricades of freed Palermo, the mysterious Doctor Calogero who eased the troubles of the sick, where Giovanni Corrao died.

"Dear old Corrao was the center, my Little One. He was the reason for all the others, I tell you. Twelve other men died that night, all of them in order to hide this one death among the many: the murder of Giovanni Corrao.

"But remember, it was not Corrao they wanted, Naguine. It was a mistake, all of it a simple case of mistaken identity. The murderers came from the mountains around Castellnotte, I'm sure. It was family, Naguine. It was blood. These men were all daggers in the employ of the Crisiani. And it was me they wanted, Naguine, it was me. All thirteen of them died because it was me they wanted dead. It was my blood on the stones they sought.

"The fools. They were confused, these hired men, and it was Corrao himself who confused them. Corrao who laughed at them, and then died in my place on those stones, where his laughter all died away to the sound of doors

78

snapping locked.   It was me, Gianni Burtoni, they wanted dead. Not Giovanni Corrao, but me.   They all died for me.

"In the papers the next day I read the list of names, the list of the thirteen dead men.   And the names, too, of some of the daggers, for the Carabinieri had rounded up two or three of them, the little daggers of Castellnotte, that cursed place, caught fleeing in the strange streets of Palermo.   I knew none of them, none except Corrao, of course.   They all were strangers, the victims and the daggers, too. Strangers, every one.

"But I knew, too, that somewhere, someone from Castellnotte was reading that list of names, just as I was. And that person, that padrone, he saw just as I did, the names of strangers in a list. But what he didn't find on that list was my name. Gianni Burtoni, the cause of it all, my name was not listed there. And I know, quietly, someone would be checking. Someone would be sent to find out if Gianni Burtoni was among those dead, under a false name. It would take them some time to do it in silence, from the inside perhaps, but someone would check those names. And then they would know that Gianni Burtoni was not there, not on the list, not among the dead.

"I did not need any more lessons, my Little One. As quietly as I could, talking to no one, not even to friends, I took the abandoned money Corrao had gotten from the train station for my work, and I left everything else behind: I needed no more persuasion.   I took the first train out of Palermo, and it carried me on a long ride across the island to Gela, and then to Ragusa. In time, I made my way on foot to Noto and then to Siracusa. From there I got work on a boat that carried me over to Taranto, and I began finally to feel I'd escaped them, and so I slowed down.

"In the papers, I watched it all from a distance. A lawyer was sent down to investigate, a man named Giacosa from Lombardy. He and the carabinieri arrested, eventually, about two dozen men, for that night that became known in the papers all across Europe as the Night of the Thirteen Daggers. Giacosa, over that bitter Sicilian winter, interrogated and investigated dozens and dozens of men, and three times men died in his custody. But no one ever talked. No one ever admitted anything, or if they came close to it, they died before they could speak. The lawyer Giacosa never even heard the name of Castellnotte, or if he did, he kept it out of the news reports.

"In the end, this Giacosa was found dead in his office. There was not a mark on him, and no cause of death could be discovered. He was slumped in his chair alone in his office, dead as the stones in the streets of the Alberghia. His desk was clean but for an unsigned form requesting his return to the North, dated on the day before he died.

"And after all of this, Giovanni Corrao was murdered with his guts spilled out on our doorstep, taking my place, murdered ignominiously and nearly alone, without an explanation, without a cause.

"Or so they say, Naguine. For I know why he died, and his death has made me homeless and alone. I am hunted still, my little Naguine, across all this time; the daggers unsheathed by Lombardo, the father of my one true love in all this world, my Rafaella, who cannot forgive my soul, they search for my heart. O Naguine, the stories I

80

could tell you. Believe me when I say this, for I know it is true. She is the one who searches still for my blood. It is she. My one heart. She and her descendants, the heirs of the blood of Lombardo spilled on the stones of a ruined cloister, filled with the remains of a ruined and beautiful garden of oranges, it is they who want to see me dead. It is she. And it is her blood."

I was alone when I awoke, Rob. The morning sun was high and warm in the sky, reaching toward noon, and its glare finally burned into my eyes. The grand sense of benevolence and unity of the whole universe from the night before was gone, and in its place I felt the painful emptiness of solitude. For a long, long while, I lay there naked in the grass under the hot sun, sweaty and thirsty, but too lethargic to rise.

It may be that I knew already what had happened, and so I didn't want to get up. But simple thirst did me in. I crawled into my pants and down to the riverbank, and drank handfuls of the cool Esino water. Some of Naguine's clothes remained, but she was gone, as I knew she would be, from the moment I awoke.

I was almost afraid to speak her name, but I called out, "Naguine?" It was really just a whisper. There was no answer. I knew there would be no answer.

With my clothes back on, and with a deep lethargy built of fear that is incipit depression, I walked back toward the camp. Of course, it was all gone. The circle of our fire, just black ashes now, was all that remained, other than a few tire tracks in the dry sand that will vanish at the first hint of breeze.

I stood there for a while, wondering blindly what to do. All I had were the clothes on my back, Rob. Naguine had left with everything else. After about an hour, when I felt a little clearer, I started to walk along the highway back into Jesi. I'd only walked for about a mile or so, when a boy on a little Japanese motorcycle pulled over, and gave me a lift into town. In Jesi, I asked after her, but to no avail. The Marchegiani of Jesi were silent, friendly, but without any news. "She'll be back," one after another of them said, sympathetic to the loss and pain in my questions. "She always comes back," they said, often enough.

But I knew better.

I wandered on into Ancona, and then Fano and Pesaro and Urbino, and even over the mountains to Gubbio. But she was gone. Many, many people knew her, remembered her well, showed me jackets and shirts she'd repaired for them. But no one knew where she had gone.

So I have rented a safe deposit box at the post office in Jesi, and I will put this history into safety, and mail you the key. And I will join the long search, Rob. I realize it now. The long search. I search for my love, Naguine of my heart. And she? She wanders I know somewhere just out of my reach, searching for her dream, for Jack Burton, the man who fascinated us as boys. Who fascinates her now. And Burton? He runs out ahead of us all, one step ahead of the daggers of the Sciascias, past the reach of the blood lust of the Crisiani, moving restlessly, always far beyond the pale, always far from Naguine, from my Naguine. He remains alone, searching for the one who long ago ordered that his ancient life be ended. He searches endlessly through time for the lost soul of love. For his Rafaella.

AFTERWORD

So ends the text that I found carefully tucked into the red folder and placed in a safe deposit box at the Postal Service in Jesi. As you can see, I have standardized the print of the last run-on pages according to the punctuation my brother added beneath his scrawled handwriting. It was nearly perfect and correct, I believe. After I finished reading, I was sitting quietly in the little room under the florescent light, when Inspector Tasso knocked once and entered.

"Is everything all right in here, Signor Roberto?" he said. "It's been quite a while."

I didn't answer right away. Then I said, "I think so." But Tasso didn't believe me, any more than I believe myself.

Over the next ten days, with a photo of my brother in my pocket and a rented Fiat Panda, I drove along the list of towns he had mentioned, and well as others on the way. In Ancona they recognized his photo at the Library, but were no help beyond that. It was the last trace of him I could find for a long while. I drove on to Fano and Pesaro, and up to

Urbino, and over to Gubbio on the old Roman road, and then even on to Perugia. Everywhere they knew of Naguine the seamstress, but no one recognized my brother from his photo. What began to haunt me was that probably his appearance had changed. This clean-cut college boy in the photo most likely bore little or no resemblance to the man I was now searching for. So he's vanished, as has this Naguine. The same way Burton has vanished, leaving legends and stories scattered all around him, but always remaining just at the periphery of my vision, and now my brother's vision, too.

Meanwhile, Postal Inspector Tasso had reported it all to the authorities. They showed my brother entering the country on his passport 90 days before. He'd stayed in a few hotels, and then vanished. They had no record of anyone named Naguine, but there was a Sofia Ziegler Pantone who carried a Bologna driver's license, married to Luigi Promoteo Pantone who had taught Eastern European languages and literature at the University. Professor Pantone claims he hadn't seen Sofia in seven years, though he remained married to her. It is probably just another dead end, but then again, perhaps not.

I called every day or so and checked in with Umberto. It's been long enough now, the inspector insists I call him Umberto. Most of the time, there is nothing more substantial for him to report than the ephemeral Signor

Pantone. But two days ago, when I called from my room in Todi, Umberto had found something.

"Roberto," he said excitedly, "I've been waiting for your call. We found him."

I braced myself for bad news, and asked "Where is he?"

"Well, at least we have a trail on him, Roberto" Tasso said. "Last Friday, someone carrying his passport took Alitalia from Naples to Palermo."

"Palermo," I said. I have to admit, it was the next step for me. If my brother was following this Naguine, and she was following Burton, then Palermo was surely on their way, sooner or later.

I reached there in a few hours on a flight out of Rome. But unfortunately, after searching for all the last week, I'm afraid every trace of him has vanished here. For a solid week, I have asked around and searched through the streets on my own, and the Palermitano Polizia have had notices out. But there is no sign. Nothing on my brother, nor Naguine, nor Jack Burton. All of it now just a strange and silent dead end.

After a week of this searching, and finding nothing but a Sicilian silence followed by a shrug, I tried to think like my brother. What would he be looking for here in Palermo? It finally occurred to me, he remains an historian at heart. So it was obvious, suddenly. Of course.

I went back to his notes, the long history he left for me, and scoured it for hints. I wandered around in the Vucciria and in the Albergheria, looking for traces of Giovanni Corrao. It was all nearly a hundred and fifty years ago, but in the Vucciria the name of Dottore Calogero still roused a smile on these staid Sicilian faces. And nearly everyone knew of the great Giovanni Corrao.

In the alleys of the Albergheria, I swear everyone I met who was older than 50 would without a moment's thought point down some narrow street and say that Corrao had lived over there. Everyone of a certain age knew where Corrao had died on the Night of the Daggers. Of course, every set of directions was different, every story I heard led to a different spot. And everyone knew for sure that this was the spot where he had died. One old woman, hanging yellowed laundry from a second floor balcony, even answered, "Right here. Signore, Dottore Calogero was murdered right here, right where you are standing. And this was his house too."

It seems that Burton and Corrao lived in nearly every other building in the whole of the Albergheria.

But still, I knew I was getting close. I could sense my brother's presence now every time I asked a question about Corrao. Yet no one recognized his photograph or his name.

Then once again the obvious occurred to me, it was my brother's training. He would not just wander around the alleys like this, asking strangers and collecting tall tales and lies. He would want to know where to look. Sure enough, I was once again right about him.

The clerk at the Palazzo di Giustizia still didn't recognize my brother's picture, but he did recognize his name. He sent me straight downstairs to the office of the tribunal archives.

They hid at the bottom of a long row of marble stairs, worn by years of use, down into the basement. The woman behind the desk was sympathetic, and she remembered him well. "It was only a week or so ago," she said. "You have the same eyes as he does, so I can see you are his family, even though you don't look much like him. Although with that long hair, and that shaggy beard, it is hard to tell."

I am clean-shaven and I still have my head razored short like in my army days. She meant to tell me, without saying as much, that my brother is no longer keeping his appearance neat.

"What did he want?" I asked her.

"Oh, that I can remember very well," she said, frowning. "I'm afraid we weren't much help to the signore. He wanted the files from an old investigation, from 1862. From a night in 1862 when thirteen men were murdered at once, in the same way, at almost the same time."

"The Night of the Daggers," I said, though in Italian it has a prettier ring when you say it. It forces you to sing, in a way. "La Notte di Pugnali," I said.

Her eyes widened, but the frown on her lips only deepened. "I see you, too, know about that night."

She was silent for a moment, gazed down at her hands and then shook her head no ever so slightly to herself, thinking I didn't notice. She muttered something in Sicilian of which I could only make out the words "blood" and "family," I think. That part I was meant to hear.

"What is it?"

"I'm afraid, Signore, we made your brother very unhappy. But it is just the way that it is here. Things get lost in all these files, do you understand? They get misplaced, filed away in the wrong place. And there is so much to keep track of here. Sometimes I'm sure it is malicious, because you know, someone wants some information to disappear. But sometimes, you know, it is just the way we are down here." Her hand reached out and dusted off the top of her desk, though it was pristinely clean and polished as it was. "I got away from here, you know, Signore. I went to library school at Sapienza, and I worked in the police archives in Rome for ten years. But then, my father passed away, and my mother was alone here in Palermo. And this job came up and, well, I had to take it, for my mother." She stopped and looked sadly in my eyes. "Things are very different down here. It can't be helped. Do you understand?"

"What are you trying to tell me?" I said.

"Signore, we searched for two days. Your brother, he came back on the second afternoon. We know from the records that there was a great investigation, it went on for months and months, Signore. There were dozens and dozens of interrogations. There must have been at least a drawer, or maybe two, filled with the files of just the main investigator. We can tell that with what our records show."

"Must have been?" I said.

She nodded, and then said, "Gone, Signore. All of it. Not one sheet of paper left. All of it, misplaced or misfiled."

"Or stolen."

"Gone," she said. "It would be harder to take it out of here, Signore, than it would be to simply bury it in all this paper."

I nodded yes. "If someone stole them, and took them out of here, they could be stolen again, perhaps easily, or just sold and then put to a different use."

She smiled that I understood. "It is easier and safer to just move the papers, change a few labels, and they disappear safely for years." We were both looking back at the rows and rows of dusty boxes stacked on shelves in the archive. "Even centuries, perhaps," she said.

"And my brother?"

"He seemed very upset, and didn't believe this was true at first. I had to take him back and show him where they were all supposed to be filed. But you can see, there are crates and crates of files stored down here, and I told him, 'Maybe they are here somewhere.' I thought he was going to get angry at first when he saw what it was. But you know, Signor Roberto, he just started to laugh. And he said something I don't understand. Perhaps you can explain it to me. He said, 'Burton's escaped again,' while he was laughing. What does it mean? 'Burton has escaped again,'"

I admit, I found myself laughing at it all too, which didn't made the archivist happy. "It's just an old friend of ours, Signora," I said. "We just can't seem to keep up with him."

I hung around in Palermo for another week or so, and I even took the picture I had and scribbled in a beard on my brother's face. It didn't do any good. Still nobody knew who he was. And still everybody claimed the house of

Dottore Calogero was right over there, right next door, right downstairs. But when that archivist told me about Will's laughter, it was a comfort. Do you understand? I knew then that my brother was okay, and in fact, I knew he was better off. He was finally out of those silly universities where he'd been hiding, and he was off into the world itself. He was searching for Jack Burton, just like me.

Before long, the call came from a drilling company. They need a 'copter pilot off the coast of Venezuela. I went back to work, knowing someday soon I would hear more.

ALSO BY SANDRO DARIOSTO

THE LAST GOOD RUN

BURTON THE RED:
An omnibus edition containing the first three adventures of
Jack Burton, including

IN THE NORTH

BURTON WITH THE THOUSAND

Forthcoming from per sempre Anita Edizione:

HANDS OF THE BIRD AND OTHER STORIES

THE WISDOM RUN

www.ingramcontent.com/pod-product-compliance
Lightning Source LLC
Chambersburg PA
CBHW070504130626
46555CB00003B/1156